# HEXED

# HEXED

Lisa Wakely

The Book Guild Ltd

First published in Great Britain in 2023 by
The Book Guild Ltd
Unit E2 Airfield Business Park,
Harrison Road, Market Harborough,
Leicestershire. LE16 7UL
Tel: 0116 2792299
www.bookguild.co.uk
Email: info@bookguild.co.uk
Twitter: @bookguild

This work is entirely fictitious and bears no resemblance to any persons living or dead.

Typeset in 12pt Minion Pro
Printed and bound in the UK by TJ Books LTD, Padstow, Cornwall

ISBN 978 1915853 745

British Library Cataloguing in Publication Data.
A catalogue record for this book is available from the British Library.

In memory of Stevie, for always believing in me and supporting my crazy adventures. Keep reaching for the stars, beautiful friend. This is for you xxx

# ONE

# VENGEANCE

*Hallows Hill, England*
*31st October 1665, year of the Black Death*

She daren't glance down at the marked trapdoor beneath her feet. A trickle of sweat raced down the bridge of her nose. Black hair whipped her face in the threatening breeze, wrapping itself around the thick rope. Rain attacked her face, soaking her black dress and forming a puddle beneath her tatty boots.

Across the town, she could see him, hiding in the shadows. Waiting for the moment that would change Hallows Hill forever. He couldn't even watch. The coward. Even though she 'repulsed' him, he couldn't bear to face the consequences of his actions. A crow shrieked. A group of them were huddled on the town wall, shifting from foot to foot impatiently.

Two minutes to go. A gust of wind blew through the dark, narrow cobbled streets, where rats scurried in the shadows. They were everywhere these days. The Ale House pub sign flapped and creaked as an empty tankard rolled into the gates of the new graveyard. She'd carved the incantations on the blank stone herself, and hidden the key underneath – for next time. The dim, yellow oil lamp outside the weaver's cottage flickered just as two horse-drawn carriages crossed each other under a stone archway. Heavy drops of rain hit the ground, splashing onto the worn cobblestones.

One minute to go. The drums rumbled to life. The crowd were still, zombie-like. He had them under his control. It was the main reason he became mayor. So that he could turn the village against her and force them to share his belief that she worshipped the devil and summoned evil spirits. One day he would learn the truth. If being able to help people with her powers made her a witch, then her confession was worth it. And that brought her here.

Any second now. The church clock ticked. The drum roll struck. *Bom. Bom. Barom bom-bom-bom. Bom. Bom. Barom bom-bom-bom.*

The church clock tolled nine o'clock.

The drum roll stopped. Silence.

She looked at him with a wounded glint in her eyes. The mayor. She pointed a finger at his shaded face and focused her mind on it and nothing else.

She swallowed. Her eyes switched from brown to a blazing orange. A burning energy twisted deep inside her gut and ripped through her heart and into her arms. It felt different this time. Painful. Magic should only be used for good, not evil, but she had no choice. It drained her of everything she had left.

"*Yersinia pestis!*" She screamed the word to inflict the Plague.

Lightning bolted from her finger, a bright jolt of it, and headed straight for his body.

The mayor jerked backwards, losing all control of his limp arms and legs. As he collapsed to the ground, the crowd drew in a gasp of shock. The scavengers didn't hesitate. Twitching their noses at the smell of new blood, a mounting number of crows and rats abandoned the Plague victims they'd been feasting on to pile on top of him, squealing in delight at the prospect of fresh food. A few seconds later, the mayor's cries faded.

"She has used her sorcery to curse him with the Plague!" The executioner pulled the creaking lever. The trapdoor flew open.

She plummeted sharply into darkness and smiled to herself. *This is not the end.*

Over in the graveyard, a dormant stone sparked and shimmered with a row of burning, lightning-white lettering. Thunder roared a startling threat. The curse was forged.

# TWO

# THE MYSTERIOUS EPITAPH

Something shifted behind the cracked gravestone at the back, the one with a man's hand carved into the top. Harriet Flynn spun around. Only two days until Halloween, one of her all-time favourite days of the year. What if it was a…

"Nope. Don't even think about it. Just get out of here," she scolded herself aloud. *Zombies and ghosts don't exist, although it'd be awesome if they did.* She'd get them to freak out all the people who got on her nerves, which happened to be most of the human race at the moment. *Nah. It was probably a fox.*

This had to be the worst shortcut ever. Deep with sludge, overgrown weeds and no light whatsoever. According to the admissions team, it was the quickest way to get to the castle. Failed to mention there wasn't any path, though, didn't they?

Harriet crouched to lift the edges of her blue dress, sopping with water and brown muck. The primroses in her wicker basket spilled onto the ground and sunk into the mud. Brilliant. If she hadn't had to run all the way back to the staffroom to collect her satchel, then she'd now be indoors like everyone else. She hadn't slept a wink last night, after Dad had left. It wasn't so much the worry for Uncle Mike but how Harriet would cope with Dad gone for the whole festival. She was completely out of her depth in Bellsbury, and Mum was always on at her to learn how to be like the other performers – loud and overconfident. Dad was the one person Harriet could trust. He understood her, he had time for her and he encouraged her to do the things that she enjoyed. He'd even tried convincing her that she could sing!

Leaves started to rustle around her. Or was that someone whispering? Harriet paused. Oh God. Without a torch, she couldn't see much of anything.

A mournful sigh floated past her ears. Her whole body stiffened. Through the rustle of leaves there came a whisper in the wind – '*Kapayi, Nihoyi. Vish hol…*', and then a stronger gust thrusted her forwards.

Grabbing her wicker basket, Harriet trudged against the wind through a sea of tangled grass and crooked gravestones.

Ouch! Her foot bashed into something rock-hard. She didn't have time to stop herself and within seconds her bottom squelched into a wet, slushy pool of mud. Just great. The wardrobe lady only washed her costume this morning and she'd made it quite clear that she wouldn't be doing another wash. What'd she wear for work tomorrow? Her pyjamas? If anyone from school found her knee-deep in mud, wearing a dress, she'd die of shame.

Still sprawled on the ground, unable to summon the energy to get up, she lifted her head of drenched hair.

The wind had died down, but before her stood a small, crumbling gravestone. It was a bit out of place among the many headstones carved with elegant epitaphs, scattered around the graveyard. This gravestone was completely blank. She shifted her bottom to stand up when a ray of moonlight splashed onto the crumbling gravestone. A single row of slanted inscription, etched with loops, flicks and tails, shone back at her.

A woman's cupped hand had been carved into the stone. *That definitely wasn't there a moment ago.*

Harriet leant further to the left, allowing the moonlight to illuminate the carved lettering.

*Kapayi, Nihoyi. Vish hol luminar vos sorcerati.*

What sort of weird language was that? The hand must've been a popular symbol in those days, it must have meant something. Was this even a grave?

Harriet dragged her knees up to her chest. Something solid pressed into her left leg; its cold, cast-iron edges scraped her bare skin. Mud seeped between her fingers as she closed her hand around the jagged object. The rusty thing looked like it'd been buried for centuries. She raked away a mound of dirt using her nails and held it upwards, twirling it from left to right until it caught a spattering of light.

A key.

It was one of those antique types with a club-shaped bow and a long stem. Its tip jutted out with two ridges that looked like a crocodile's jaw. Harriet twisted the key again. At the top, on the bow, were etched a clutter of letters. Four letters? No, three letters. Yes, three.

"H-H-O... no, B... or is that a D?" Harriet scrunched her eyes and held the key up against her nose.

Below the letters were six numbers. *311065*. Could that be a date, or perhaps someone's phone number?

What if the key was connected to the gravestone? She could've found something here, a genuine antique. Harriet reached into her satchel and wrapped her grimy fingers around her phone. The stone wasn't exactly captivating, but it was an interesting subject. As long as she had a clear shot of the engraving, she'd be able to Google it later.

Several bugs scuttled across the gravestone, just as the clock in the church tower chimed eight times. A tornado of crisp leaves whizzed through the graveyard and Harriet wriggled her shoulders. A heavy cloud rolled over the moon, dulling its bright rays.

The carved eulogy disappeared. Perhaps it was designed to glow in the dark?

There came that rustling noise again, from over by the bushes. Harriet turned her head, her pulse racing. Slipping the key into her dress pocket, she ran. Weeds snatched at her ankles as she followed the long path out of the centuries-old graveyard, passing the Fair where the old stake used for burning criminals stood tall. Her soggy shoes smacked onto an empty cobbled-stoned street littered with wooden barrels and crates. The pong of decomposing fruit combined with coal smoke zipped up her nose.

*Mm, very authentic. Jorvic Centre, eat your heart out.*

Orange lights flickered behind the windows of thatched pubs, where the buzz of conversation flooded the air.

*At last.* Just beyond that stone archway stood Bellsbury Castle, its grandness half-lit by yellow spotlights against the jet-black sky. It looked a bit like one of the castles she'd seen in those old *Dracula* films that Dad watched practically all the time. Its several towers and turrets could probably be seen all the way from the next town in Dorset. Apparently, it belonged to King James I back in the 1600s – or something like that. She probably should've paid more attention during the mini history lesson on training day, but what was the point in learning about stuff that no longer exists?

Harriet stepped into the wide entrance hall and dragged her grubby shoes along the cold stone floor. She hated it being quiet like this. All she could hear were her own footsteps squelching towards the huge staircase at the bottom of the hall. Halfway up, the staircase spiralled to the left and the right. Choosing the left staircase, she took a slow walk up the uneven hard steps. Using an old castle as accommodation for staff and guests was a pretty cool idea. Although having to sacrifice modern-day light for battery-operated candles totally sucked. Especially when the battery ran out while you were on the loo.

It was such a shame Dad wouldn't get to see his seventeenth-century festival come to life. He'd spent so many late nights planning it. But last night Aunt Michelle had called from France: Uncle Mike was in a diabetic coma, and could Dad come as soon as possible? Mum insisted he be with his brother, 'just in case'. That left Mum and Dad's assistant, Ben Jennings, in charge of everything.

In charge of each other more like. These next three days would be absolute torture. But at the same time, it'd mean no arguments between Mum and Dad for a while.

Harriet let out a breath when she reached the third floor. The staff bedchambers took up this whole floor. At last. Room number 407.

Twisting the accommodation key in the small arched door, Harriet stepped into the large, wood-panelled lounge where she also slept. Paintings of old royalty (no idea who they were) and tapestries covered the stone walls. Fake wax candles flickered by the window. Harriet tossed her empty basket onto a chair, letting out a loud, deliberate grumble. Her roommate and best friend from school, Liliana Garcia – Lily – was so fascinated in something on her laptop that she hadn't seen Harriet. Bet it was a boy, had to be.

Harriet peered over her shoulder. Oh, would you look at that. Lily was on Facebook – again. Stalking a boy. *Wayne Barry.* Yes, OK, those ice-blue eyes were super dreamy. Oh, and that silver stud in his right ear looked cool. Wayne had been employed as a jester at Bellsbury. He totally rocked that role.

"He's only in the room next door, you know," Harriet teased.

Lily slammed the laptop shut and spun around, pulling a face. "Shh, he'll hea… Ew, what is happening to you, my lovely?"

"I decided to have a bath in the graveyard," Harriet moaned, washing her hands in a basin of soapy water. The key she'd found in the graveyard swung forwards in her pocket, thumping against the basin.

"What is that being in your pocket?" Lily had never lost her Spanish twang.

"I found an old key by a weird gravestone." Harriet delved into her satchel and pulled out her phone, enlarging the photo of the epitaph – if you could even call it that. "I took a photo of it. Come and see."

Lily had to be Harriet's biggest photography fan and always made a point to 'like' all her photos on Facebook and Instagram before anyone else got there, to prove she was her best friend.

Lily used her slender fingers to stretch the image. "Where are you seeing this gravestone?"

"Here. In Bellsbury."

"No, I don't think so."

"I tripped over it. It's definitely there."

"No, I mean I am thinking it is not real. I don't even know this language. What is *vish hol* meaning?" Lily used a wet thumb to smear a patch of mud from Harriet's forehead.

Harriet shrugged. "The words only showed up in the moonlight too. I've never seen a gravestone like it." But the key was definitely old, and she was sure they were linked.

"It is not like any language I am seeing before, but the carved hand symbol is popular. Usually it is a man and woman's hand being clasped together. It represents unity in life and death. I have never seen just the one hand, though. Maybe it has been broken from the man's hand?" Lily pirouetted out of her seat to practise her country dancing, which she helped the dance tutor to teach during the day. Even though she was sixteen, the same age as Harriet, she was so small that people mistook her for a ten-year-old. She had more energy than one too.

"Harri!" Lily's shrill voice pierced through Harriet's ears.

Lily stared at a massive black ball dangling from her hand. Tears poured from her wide eyes and she flapped her hand around like a maniac.

"Get it away from me! I don't like it. Get it out! Get it out!" Lily screamed, clutching the rosary beads hanging around her neck. Wow, she had some lungs on her. "*¡Dios me salve!* It is looking at its reflection in my glasses."

Harriet edged as far back from the spider as possible. Just looking at it gave her the creeps, but no way would she admit to it. "Please stop screaming."

Lily made a jumble of peculiar noises and leaped onto the nearest chair, eyes growing wider as the spider shifted onto her chest. Something hard kicked against the door.

Harriet spun around.

The door flung open and whacked against the wall.

# THREE

# THE JESTER AND THE BARBER SURGEON

Oh my God.

The boy they'd just been ogling on Facebook was standing in their doorway. His hooded ice-blue eyes and crooked smile reminded Harriet of a Hollywood actor she fancied. He had dirty blond hair styled into a messy Mohican. Behind him, his roommate Tyrone Stiles – a lanky guy around sixteen, with a small bobbly nose and dark, shaven hair – stood gaping at the girls. Hands in the pockets of his green woolly jumper, Tyrone's mouth hung slightly open – a total contrast to his persona as barber surgeon.

"What you two doing in here?" Wayne Barry spoke in a husky East London accent. He glanced from Lily quaking on the chair to Harriet standing r, caked in mud. He looked Harriet up before acknowledging her with a nod. "If ou feel any better, my dog suffered from ace too. Used to wear a nappy, he did."

He said it completely deadpan, making the joke without blinking or changing his facial expression and tone of voice. For some reason, Harriet couldn't look back at him.

"This is m-mud," Harriet stuttered. *Where'd this speech impediment come from all of a sudden?* Her stomach flipped over and over. She'd never been great at talking to boys. What exactly did boys like talking about? Cars? Girls? Computer games? Ugh. To avoid any further awkwardness, she pointed to her helpless friend. "Erm, could you please get rid of the spider?"

"Sure," said Wayne, fidgeting with his peaked fringe. He smiled up at Lily. "Hey, mate."

"Get this thing and all its legs away from me! I think it is actually Satan," she said, keeping as still as a statue, her arms posed at odd angles.

"*Hello, Wayne, how are you? Not bad, ta. How are you?*" Wayne muttered to himself in an animated manner. He pulled up a chair beside Lily and bounded on top of it, regarding her odd posture before copying it. "What we doing? Yoga?"

Lily started giggling, but as she breathed out the spider moved across her chest. She screamed. "This is witchcraft. Get it away from me, *Yaya*. Please!"

Wayne threw a vacant look behind him. "What did you just call me?"

"*Yaya.* Sorry, she is my grandma." Lily squealed as her chair wobbled.

"I've been called worse." Wayne grabbed the back of her chair with a firm hand.

Lily bounced on her toes, breathing erratically. "Please, you get this devil worshipper away from me."

"Yes, sir." Wayne saluted. He spent a few seconds staring at the spider before grasping it with his fingers. He held it up to Lily's face. From its middle, he tugged out a strand of black hair, then another, then another until it'd disintegrated into nothing.

*Oh for God's sake, Lily.* Harriet let her head flop forwards.

"You've got to be kidding. I didn't realise how blind you were!" This wasn't the first time she'd found Lily's hair tangled up in random objects. "Lils, you need to do something about your hair. It's all over the place."

Wayne leaped down from the chair. "How about running a lawnmower over her head?"

Lily stared at the ground, muttering in Spanish. One of her favourite sayings – 'life's too short to get embarrassed' – clearly didn't apply right now. Funny how things suddenly changed when there were boys around.

Tyrone was still standing in the exact same spot, gaping up at Lily in that same way. "What language is that? Are you German?"

Lily caught her breath back and looked at Tyrone with the widest eyes humanly possible. "German? No, I am Spanish. I come from La Saida in Valencia. Are you from the land of stupid?"

Tyrone screwed up his eyes. "OK, so what am I saying then? *Je n'ai plus de papier toilette.*"

"I don't know because it is French, you idiot!" Lily snapped.

"Apparently he's run out of toilet paper." Wayne waggled his eyebrows at Tyrone.

Tyrone scowled. "Whatever. Why are these girls so touchy?"

The room fell silent. Harriet couldn't bear awkward silences; but it was Lily who sprung in to divert the conversation. "Harri, show the boys what you find in the graveyard."

Why'd Lily have to mention the photo? It was pretty weird, to take a photo of an old gravestone. But she'd been really getting into her photography recently, often of dark, empty spaces – random churches, bridges and empty London streets. It didn't mean she wanted to share them, though.

Harriet grunted under her breath. She didn't exactly have a choice now. "As I was walking back through the churchyard, I found an old gravestone. It had the weirdest inscription I've ever seen. There were no names or dates, but I found a key beside it. Have a look."

Wayne and Tyrone stepped either side of Harriet,

leaning closer to study the photo on her phone screen. As Wayne's chest brushed against her shoulder, a strong scent of sandalwood and fresh spices wafted up her nose. He was quite stocky compared to Tyrone. Oh God. An entire colony of worms wriggled around her stomach so quickly that she could barely breathe. The sensible thing to do would be to move out of his way, but she couldn't. Or rather, she didn't want to.

Tyrone used his fingers to zoom in and out of the photo on the screen. "You know what I reckon? It might not be a gravestone. It might be… a cake. Y'know, in disguise."

*What?* Harriet remembered Tyrone coming out with some bizarre statements during the training day too, the weirdest being, "You smell like my aunt's carpet," or, "I was a lot younger when I was born." People seemed to accept it and laugh. Right now all she could do was peer up at Wayne.

He leant into her and spoke from the corner of his mouth. "Just say nothing. Hopefully it'll go away."

Tyrone folded his arms.

Harriet cleared her throat noisily and removed the key from her pocket. "Look at this. Lily thinks it's a prop, but I reckon the gravestone is connected to this key."

Tyrone peered closely at the key, knitting his brows. "It might be a fake key to the castle. Look, there're some letters on here. H-H-D. Hmm. Harriet's Hair Disaster?"

Wayne snorted, holding the tip of the key with his fingers. "What makes you think the key is connected to the gravestone?"

Harriet could already detect a hint of doubt in his voice. "Both the key and the gravestone look centuries old. It can't be a coincidence that I found them within inches of each other."

"Yeah, but both our nans probably look centuries old; don't mean they're related though, does it?" Wayne raised his eyebrows in question.

Harriet pretended not to hear Tyrone crack up with laughter. Why were boys so annoying?

"The key is just a toy for children to find." Lily sighed. Straightening her glasses, she rested her chin on Harriet's shoulder. "How are you saying these words on the gravestone? They are not English, no?"

Was there even a right way to say the words? Harriet tapped the screen to make it light up again, holding her phone watch by the beam of moonlight shining in through the window. For a moment, the words on the gravestone appeared English: *We must all be at one for us to rest. Mine is his. His is mine. Our bones shall rest together.* She stared hard at the words until her phone screen annoyingly flicked off. Grunting aloud, she moved away from the window and tapped the screen to view the photo once again. The strange non-English words reappeared. Perhaps it'd been a trick of the eye.

"Go on. Read it out then!" Tyrone pressed her.

Harriet shook away her confusion and focused on the words. "*Kapayi, Nihoyi. Vish hol luminar vos sorcerati.*"

The others repeated her, trying out their own pronunciations. The expression on everyone's face was funnier than the verse itself.

"What do you think it means?" Lily asked, when they'd stopped giggling over it. Harriet considered telling them about the English words she'd briefly seen, but she couldn't decide whether it'd just been her imagination. Besides, she'd forgotten what most of it said – something about resting together.

Outside, the bell in the church tower chimed nine times.

With the last chime, the shutters swung back on their hinges. Wind stormed through the window. The bottle of holy water that Lily's grandmother had given her, toppled onto the hard floor, smashing into a million pieces. The candles tipped over and crashed to the ground. Blackness veiled the room.

"There was nothing on the weather about a hurricane tonight," said Harriet. She tapped her way around the room, hunching her quaking shoulders when she reached the window. Clasping the levers, she wrestled the window shut before the wind could slam it on her fingers.

Nine o'clock already? Tomorrow morning she'd become a primrose seller again, if she could find a decent costume. When would she find the time to figure out where the key had come from and what the gravestone was all about? It wasn't a toy or a prop. The others were wrong. Dad could probably tell her, being into history and all. Although did finding an old grave really warrant calling someone while they were at their brother's hospital bedside? *I just miss you, Dad*, Harriet sighed.

She switched on another set of candles and grabbed a dustpan and brush from behind the bin, helping the others to sweep up the shards of broken glass scattered on the floor. If Mum saw this mess she'd go spare. She'd probably blame Harriet for not closing the window properly. Once the room looked decent enough, she sat and stared at the verse in some weird hope that the words would suddenly translate to English again.

Tyrone shrugged. "Forget about it, man. It's just a prop, like the key."

"You weren't there to see the actual gravestone. I know that the props team wouldn't have touched the graveyard out of respect. The key must've been lying there for centuries," she hit back.

What did he know? He didn't care. None of them did. Well, whatever. She'd find out about that grave and key with or without their help, especially as the same question kept humming around her mind. What if she'd found a real historical artefact?

# FOUR

# THE NIGHTMARE

Harriet switched off the bedside candle and bounced into her bed, listening to the castle creak and groan. The window rattled in its corroding frame. Tree branches smacked and clawed at the glass. Beneath her, the mumble of conversation stopped. Everyone but Harriet was asleep.

The rustle of clothing swept along the passage.

*Someone's up late*, she mused.

The floorboard outside her room groaned. Footsteps shuffled beneath the gap under the door. Harriet nestled under the duvet. A fist pounded against her door. It wasn't the normal rap rap. It sped up to about one thousand knocks per minute. No human could knock that quickly. Harriet gripped the duvet so hard that her knuckles started to shake. This wasn't normal.

It stopped.

Heavy wood brushed against the matted rug inside the room. Had she forgotten to lock the door?

"Hello?" Harriet could barely manage a whisper. Surely Lily could hear all this from her separate bedchamber on the other side of the wall? Though if she could sleep through violent hailstorms then she could sleep through anything.

A musky air clogged her throat. A spicy, herbal smell floated up her nose. Something that might've been dry sand trickled onto her face. Harriet coughed. A lump the size of a football grew in the pit of her stomach. Somebody was in her room. Watching her. Her heart pumped double its normal speed.

Swallowing hard, she counted to six and mumbled, "Lily?" But the voice that responded didn't belong to Lily. It didn't even sound human.

"*Keep the treasure, it will protect you, but one. Follow the signs that will guide you there. Silas has returned from the grave. For you. Beware the curse.*" The strange whoosh of echoes continued. "*The gift I am to give you – you must keep it. It will reveal itself by morning. Save me, save yourselves.*"

"Wh-who's there?" Harriet bolted upright.

A silvery light beamed through a gap in the curtains, spilling light over half the room. All she could see were the outline of books, furniture, bags. Not a person. Someone had been in here. She'd sensed it, felt their presence, smelt their breath, heard their voice. Maybe it was one of those dreams-within-a-dream type of thing, where you wake up, but you're still dreaming.

Harriet reached for the candlestick beside her bed and switched on the flickering light. A nippy draught slipped through the cracks in the window. She slipped into her spotted nightgown and tiptoed over to the door, peering through the gap into the passageway. Something was drawing her on, telling her to follow.

*It's only a dream, Harri.*

Royal-sounding Baroque music filtered up the stairs and coasted through Harriet's open door. The music had a hint of sadness about it. Who was playing? She had to know.

A cloud of mist drifted from her lips, evaporating into the hard, stone walls where candle flames flickered in their holders. Any colder and she'd freeze to death.

*It's only a dream.*

Harriet trod cautiously down the winding staircase, trying her best not to make a sound. The harpsichord grew louder, sharper, clearer after each step, streaming through a tiny gap in the drawing-room door. This room always remained locked at night, so how had this person managed to get in?

Now that she was standing right outside the door, she could hear fingers tapping the harpsichord keys, making use of every note with incredible speed. She poked her head through the gap.

The music stopped mid-tune. All the lights were out.

Was this some kind of wind-up? All of a sudden, Harriet felt very, very awake.

She pushed the door wide open and marched inside. She waved the candle through the air. Just paintings and rugs, old furniture and a harpsichord that looked like it hadn't been touched in decades. Whoever was in here must've run out.

The temperature dropped.

Every window and mirror fogged up, then the room dissolved into darkness. Harriet turned to face the door. The batteries for these candles were useless. Whenever they'd had power cuts at home, Tasha always switched on a torch and held it beneath her chin because she knew it'd make Harriet scream. As much as she hated her older sister sometimes, she kind of wished she was here right now. Not only was it now pitch black, but a strong waft of fresh earthiness prickled her throat. She bit her tongue. Something heavy dragged across the floor. Similar to the sound she'd heard outside her bedroom door earlier.

"Hello?" Harriet whispered, using her less shaky hand to grapple around for the emergency room light. Stupid thing wasn't there.

Water trickled towards Harriet's feet, soaking her toes. The dragging stopped. Harriet's insides clenched up. Somebody, or something, was stood a few inches behind her. Oh God. She couldn't stand here forever.

It had to be one of the actors. Harriet turned around.

Lightning struck outside the window, illuminating the room briefly.

A woman stared back at her. Water dribbled from every hole in her long-faded black dress. A rainy puddle formed around her tatty black boots.

Harriet stiffened, letting out a small shriek. Sweat pricked the back of her neck.

Lightning flashed again.

Coarse, sodden black hair clung to the greyish-white skeletal face. Several bugs crawled out from the black eye sockets and disappeared through a deep gash in her cheek. The muskiness that seeped from her clothing grew so strong that Harriet felt like she was standing in her garden.

The woman jerked her head upwards to speak. Her voice was deep and scratchy.

"*I bestow to you, the powers for which I was killed.*

"*The primrose seller shall prune the tender thorns.*

"*The jester shall perform others' wishes.*

"*The dancer will court flames, storm and stream.*

"*The barber shall learn to shape time itself.*

"*Emotion and unity will ignite their strength.*"

The woman glided closer, her face merely centimetres from Harriet's.

"*Bury the bones, together, before the ninth hour on Halloween night. I was hidden, in fear of the magic coming to light. Use the key to open the iron cage beneath your feet, where bugs feast on human meat.*

*Beware Silas. Your choice will influence how it ends. Betrayal is upon you.*"

Harriet found herself nodding, even though none of this made sense. It took her a few seconds to find her weak voice. "W-what will happen if I don't bury these bones?" Behind Harriet, the drawing-room door slammed shut. Her legs refused to move from the spot.

The woman's skeletal features looked a hundred times more frightening close up. "*You shall perish, becoming part of the curse, reliving your death. One little villager hanging from the noose, nobody there to cut them loose... May God have mercy on your soul.*"

"Please stop! I'll do it. I'll bury the bones before nine on Halloween night! Please leave me alone," Harriet screamed, and whirled around to face the door. Who was this woman standing behind her? Was she an actress paid to scare the staff as well as the guests? Was it Wayne or Tyrone messing about? What had Harriet just agreed to do?

Her questions could wait. Harriet grabbed the door handle and forced it up and down. *Open, you stupid thing.* Sweat gathered on the palm of her hands. How could the door be locked? She came in this way!

Harriet paused. Apart from the ticking of a small clock on the shelf, the room was now silent. She closed her eyes briefly. *Is it over?*

Biting her lip, Harriet let her hand slide from the door handle and turned around in three tiny steps.

A dark shadow breathed cold, earthy air into her face, the woman's skeletal outline barely a centimetre away. Two hollow eye sockets glared right at her.

Harriet stumbled backwards, her back crashing hard into the door. She wasn't sure what made her say it out loud, but she mumbled, "Please don't kill me."

This woman could be an escaped convict or a wanted murderer or something. There was a prison about fifteen miles from here.

After a long silence, the woman flung her head to one side so violently that the top of her head hit her shoulder. Bones cracked and snapped. Flesh ripped and squished. The woman gurgled.

*What the...* Harriet's heart beat through her ears. This was way too real. If she didn't carry out the woman's instruction, is that what would happen to her? She spun back to the door and fumbled around for the handle.

A withered arm reached over her shoulder towards the door.

*Come on, come on, open*, Harriet pleaded, yanking the handle up and down.

The door swung open.

Harriet gasped in relief, tripping out of the drawing room in a mad panic. She couldn't tell whether it was feet pacing behind her or the hall clock ticking, but she daren't turn around. The never-ending spiral staircase proved a lot more difficult to run up in the dark and she had to clutch the handrail to help guide her to the top, but eventually she reached room 407.

Somewhere behind her, footsteps padded up the stairs.

"Just go away, whoever you are," Harriet called over her shoulder, and burst through the door. For the first time, she used the latch and propped a nearby chair against the door for extra measure.

"Lils! Lily!" she cried, jiggling the handle up and down on Lily's chamber door. Damn grandparents' rule!

She leaped into her bed and pulled the duvet over her head. She didn't feel safe in her warm bed anymore. How could she sleep now? Morning couldn't come quick enough.

# FiVE

# A GIFT FROM THE PAST

Harriet breathed out a yawn. She'd eventually sunk into a broken sleep after leaping back into bed. The weird visions of a girl dangling from a noose kept waking her up. The face had been blurry, but her body frame indicated her young age. She'd worn trousers and a thick winter coat, a bit like Harri's one with the Eskimo hood.

So what had really happened last night? The woman's deathly pale face slipped right back into Harriet's mind. And then there was the sand from the figure in her room… and the task.

Actually, there wasn't any trace of sand in her bed. And the harpsichord – she'd just remembered that it wasn't a real harpsichord. Dad had bought a replica for display purposes. You couldn't play anything on it, which proved that it must've been a dream. Just a seriously intense dream. "Harri, come on. We have only half an hour before the morning briefing is starting and we are still in our pyjamas," Lily shrieked from next door.

Half an hour? Harriet flung on her dressing gown and raced into the bathroom, wading through a large muddy puddle in the centre of the room. How did that get there? Had it rained through the window last night? Thank goodness the water wasn't any deeper. She'd never been a confident swimmer like her sister. Deep water scared her, especially when her feet couldn't reach the bottom. She usually pulled 'sickies' on the days she had swimming lessons at school.

There wasn't any time to clear up the mess right now. Stepping out of the puddle, Harriet leant over the sink. She splashed a handful of water onto her face and looked into the steamy mirror.

The reflection that stared back at her wasn't her face.

Where the eyes should be were two sunken holes. From the corners of the mouth seeped a trail of dark red blood that stained the greyish-white skin. The blistered lips, stitched together with thick black thread, ripped apart, revealing five rotted teeth. A voice in her head rasped, *Silas is back. Use the key. Find the bones. Prevent your death.*

Someone or something started humming the harpsichord tune that Harriet heard last night. It was so loud, it could have come from her mouth, but that would be impossible. Oh heck. Harriet stumbled backwards, letting out a small cry. Visions of that woman came flooding back. *Please, go away.* She closed her eyes for ten seconds, struggling to control her manic heartbeat with deep breathing. Clenching her sweaty fists, Harriet prised open her eyes, straining to see through the fine layer of mist now coating the mirror. Oh God. Using her fingertips, she dabbed at the condensation.

Then she saw it. The reflection: tangled long copper red hair, annoying red spot on her forehead that refused to bugger off, a gathering of freckles running over her nose, more than five slightly uneven but not rotten teeth and a small mole on the right cheek. Harriet blinked at her reflection. The jaded blue eyes in the mirror blinked back.

What the...? She spun around. The large puddle of water had gone. The humming had stopped. But that face – it'd looked exactly like the one she saw last night. All the more reason to hurry up, bathe and get out.

It turned out to be the quickest bath she'd ever had. What should've taken fifteen minutes took less than five. It didn't help hearing Lily's countdown to the morning briefing from her small bedchamber in the room next door.

Harriet's panic levels were already high enough without Lily adding to it. Twice she dropped her hairbrush, and she must've knocked her phone watch into the bin three or four times. Her hands hadn't stopped shaking since last night. Now she just felt sick.

Harriet turned to her bed. Couldn't she just crawl back in and hide under the covers? Surely everything that'd happened would go away – if only for a while. Those hopes didn't last for long. Not when she spotted something on her bed that wasn't there before.

A book.

Where'd that come from? She edged closer to the book and sat beside it on the bed. "*The History of Hallows Hill*," she mumbled the title. She could just about see the faded lettering on the tatty front cover. The book looked older than her ancient head teacher, its pages yellower than his teeth. Whoever put the book on her bed must've done so really cautiously. It was thicker than an encyclopaedia with pages that would probably fall out if she picked it up.

Why would someone assume she needed to know the history of Hallows Hill? It's what Bellsbury Village used to be called, in the 1600s or something. That's all she needed to know, right?

"Lils?" Harriet yelled, waiting for some kind of response from her friend. Finally, Lily made a grunting noise. "Did you leave a history book on my bed?"

"¿Qué?" Lily called back.

"Did. You. Leave. A. History. Book. On. My. Bed?"

Harriet realised she probably sounded patronising, but she wasn't in the mood for games right now.

"A history book? No, I am leaving nothing on your bed. I would like you to hurry up so we are not being late," Lily shouted back. She mumbled something else that sounded like, "You don't read books."

That ruled her out. So if it wasn't Lily, who put this book on Harriet's bed while she was in the bathroom?

A blue tasselled bookmark poked out from the halfway point. Harriet stared at it for a moment until curiosity won over.

### Hallows Hill Gaol and Dungeons

*Hallows Hill Gaol is one of the oldest working gaols in the country, dating back to 1500. It was the scene of numerous executions, including the last in Dorset in 1665, and is said to be haunted by the spirit of its final prisoner, Mohana Oakes. On plans dating back a hundred years, archaeologists discovered secret passageways below the gaol where they found a lost dungeon hidden beneath the former gaol yard. Archaeologists reported they found a way to the secret dungeon by removing iron covers. They believe the bones of the final prisoner can be found within a cage. Paranormal experts have warned that an ancient curse should befall he who disturbs the dead. Beware!*

She realised that her heart had started racing. Her eyes darted to the main door. A ray of light fell through the small gap between the door and the frame. Someone had been in here. Or had she forgot to lock it last night? Her conscience assured her that she'd planted a chair against the door. If she had, it wasn't there now. Didn't that freaky woman in black mention something about iron and a cage last night? She was in the bathroom earlier. She must've put this book on Harriet's bed to remind her about the task. Could there be a link between the woman and this historic information? Who was Mohana Oakes? And that year, 1665. That was the same year as the Plague: the only historic event that'd been drilled into Harriet's head at primary school. If Harriet did the task, would this woman stop visiting and threatening her? She considered slipping the book under her bed and forgetting about this whole thing. What's the worst that could happen? She stopped, remembering the words from last night: "*You shall perish, becoming part of the curse, reliving your death.*" Harriet closed her eyes, berating herself for agreeing to do something she knew nothing about. She hadn't a clue where to start. Did that mean someone was going to kill her? Was it just an empty threat?

"Harri! Are you ready now?" Lily called from her room.

Harriet flipped open her eyes. She realised she was still in her pyjamas. The costume she'd worn yesterday now drooped over the lau..., stained with dried mud and grass. She'd nev... it to the costume store before the briefing. Wha... heck was she going to wear?

*

"You look very lovely." Lily couldn't lie to save her life.

Harriet pulled the white linen sheet further around her shoulders. It wasn't exactly fitting for the seventeenth-century period, but according to Lily, it was fitting for Halloween. So here she was, walking down Fortune Street, ready for her day's work... dressed as a ghost. Lily had made her a costume out of a used bedsheet; it had uneven holes for eyes. Through them, Harriet could see that the market sellers were already muttering to one another and sniggering at her. It felt just like being back at school.

Harriet didn't really have many friends there either, apart from Lily and two other girls called Becky and Claire. Actually, Becky had just started hanging out with the loud girls from their class. Now she wore make-up and barely spoke to Harriet. Clearly cosmetics gave some girls the right to be complete cows.

A horse and cart thundered past. Its iron wheels grated along the cobbles. Harriet jolted backwards, clasping Lily's arm.

' said Lily. She blew a double
nilkmaid, who returned the
d by, carrying a pair of churns

ier mouth to answer but choked
rm animals and rotting fish that
gy air. Instead, she replied with a
half-hea...

It felt like Dad had been planning this three-day festival village ever since Harriet had been small. He totally loved history, especially the Stuart era, and wanted to recreate the sights and smells of that particular period for people to experience. He'd hired loads of actors and retail staff who had to attend a training day to learn their craft and how to speak Elizabethan English. For Harri, it brought back memories of reciting Shakespeare at school.

One guest said it felt like walking inside the pages of a history book! They could just wander into real homes, watch the seamstress embroidering clothing for the wealthy, chat to the weaver or help the potter firing up his kiln. Harriet had never felt so proud of Dad.

The morning briefing for the Performers team was being held on the lower floor of the weaver's cottage. Good. Because the stairs in that cottage were a danger to anyone in heels, massive bedsheets or society in general. Harriet tottered through the entrance, her clogs clanking along the crooked timber floorboards.

The team leader's muffled voice greeted the team in the main room ahead.

Lily prodded Harriet's back. "Come on, chick, move quicker."

"Yes. All right." Harriet knocked over a display of seventeenth-century fabrics as she barged into the dwelling quarters.

Differently dressed actors and dancers sat in various spots around the room listening to the team leader who, Harriet realised, had now stopped talking to stare at her. Actually, everyone's eyes were focused on Harriet, looking up and down the white sheet wrapped around her entire body. Her leg trembled like it always did in front of a large crowd. She couldn't think of anything funny to say to break the silence. Instead, she followed Lily and sat down in the gap behind Wayne and Tyrone.

The jester, in his motley jingly waistcoat, breeches and two-pointed hat covered with bells, peered around and blew a low wolf-whistle. Little did he realise how much that turned Harriet's insides into mush, regardless of it being intended as a joke. He considered Harriet's outfit thoughtfully, knitting his brows. The girl with her head on his shoulder didn't bother looking at Harriet but smirked to herself. Jazz combed back her short peroxide hair. How she'd got a job in a kids' club, with such a stinking attitude, was just baffling.

"Don't even say it," Harriet groaned, eyes darting everywhere.

"Say what?" Wayne held his hands up, widening his eyes like a disobedient child pretending to look innocent. "So any reason why you've come dressed as a bed?"

Harriet bit her lips to hide a grin. Why did he have to half-smile at her like that? It did funny things to the colour of her face.

The team leader slurped his tea and rambled on about the amount of guests in the village, special praise for several staff and ending the speech with, "Smile, team, it's going to be an awesome-tacular day, dot com." Where did Mum find these people? Actually, where was a bucket when you needed one?

Harriet didn't feel too confident about it being an *awesome-tacular day*, whatever that meant. Not now that she had an impossible task to complete.

# SiX

# THE WARNING

A furious buzz of activity filled the room as everyone gathered their props and moved in droves towards the door to take their positions in the village, some glancing back to snigger at Harriet before leaving the cottage.

"Harri, ignore them. They are just being jealous." Lily shimmied over to Harriet and paused. "Are you OK, lovely? You look tired."

Harriet doubted that the team were jealous about the fact she was wearing a bedsheet, but she chose not to say anything. "I had a weird dream last night."

"Really? Me too. What was your dream about?" Lily leant a chin on Harriet's shoulder.

Harriet couldn't imagine that Lily's dream was anywhere near as frightening as her dream – if it was a dream. "I dreamt about a woman."

"Lucky you." Wayne perched cross-legged on the edge of the display table and began to juggle five small balls. "Was she naked?"

Harriet pretended not to hear him. "This woman had about five mouldy teeth and her lips were all blistered. At first I thought it was you and Tyrone trying to scare me."

"Yeah, I can see how you might mistake two teenage boys for an old lady. People confuse me with my nan all the time." Wayne hunched his shoulders and jutted out his bottom jaw. He glanced over at Tyrone and the two of them laughed. He turned his attention back to Harriet. "This woman. Did she look like some kind of prehistoric nun with no eyes? That's the stunner I dreamt about last night."

Wait. What? For once, Harriet couldn't tear her eyes away from Wayne. This had to be some kind of joke. She tried to blink.

"So... so are you saying you saw her too?"

"Who? Your mum?" Wayne slowly shrunk backwards at Harriet's glare. He exchanged glances with Tyrone and chuckled. "What?"

Lily's mouth had swung open. She clamped both hands on Wayne's cheeks. "¡Dios mío! No, you are making up big lies. Are you talking about a different zombie woman to the one I see last night?"

"What?" Harriet blurted out. Surely Lily didn't have the same dream?

Wayne fixed Lily with a tight smile. "No idea what

you just said, but sure."

"Did you see her at the same time I was seeing her?" Lily's breathing had become erratic.

"See who, you lunatic?" Wayne leant away from her.

"The goat woman," Lily whined.

"The what woman?"

"You know, *NEIGH*."

"That's a horse."

Lily pulled Wayne's hands back and forth. "I am talking about *the* woman. D-did she say anything?"

"Fudge sake. You're mental. Do you mean the woman in my dream?" Wayne looked more confused than anything else. "She said something about a treasure protecting me. Why?"

Tyrone's head jolted upwards at this. He let his phone slip to the floor.

*No way.* This had to be a joke. Harriet froze. How? How could this be possible? How could three people have the same dream at the same time?

Lily squealed, holding on to the rim of her glasses. "I don't believe it. Wayne, this is a big shock!"

"I know, right?" Wayne slowly nodded his head, eyes narrowed. "...Genuinely don't know what you're talking about, mate."

"I dream about the same thing – about the woman," Lily stammered. She closed her eyes for a couple of seconds. "I dream about a zombie woman. It was feeling so real. I could smell her. Think 'goat who doesn't wear deodorant' smell. She put lots of dirt on me. She say something about a gift revealing itself by morning."

"What the…?" Wayne said a four-letter word that made Lily gasp in shock and mutter an apology to the ceiling, clutching her rosary beads. "That's trippy. I mean, there weren't no goats, but there was a zombie woman."

Harriet wanted to be sick. She could understand it if they'd all watched a film or read a book about a morbidly dressed woman, but none of them had time for books or TV at Bellsbury.

Tyrone cracked his knuckles one by one. Awful noise. He'd been pacing up and down the room but stopped dead in the centre, making odd whimpering sounds.

*Please don't say he's had the same dream too.* But his expression didn't look promising.

"Was this woman's hair black? Like, jet-black? Because I dreamt about her too. But, you know, maybe it's one of those dreams where it was her, but it wasn't her. You know what I mean? Like once, I dreamt I was in my house, but then it turned into the school library and my teacher was my dad, but then he turned into an ape."

Wayne's eyes wandered sideways. "Not gonna lie – bit weird."

Harriet picked at a ball of wool on the table beside her. Weren't dreams predictions of the future? Or so she'd read in some magazine. But then what about this morning? Last night couldn't have been a dream, which meant the woman had actually been in their room. She cleared her throat. "I... I saw that woman again in the bathroom mirror earlier. It was her face instead of mine."

"That's called your reflection." Tyrone chuckled, clicking his fingers. "Try wearing some make-up before you look in the mirror next time."

"You're such an idiot. I'm guessing none of you saw her this morning, otherwise you would've said something, right?" Harriet bit her lip. They answered with blank expressions and prolonged silences, looking at her as though she'd just made the whole thing up. Except for Wayne, whose eyes remained on the ground. None of them had mentioned the task about the whole burying the bones thing. Then again, none of them had seen the strange woman in the drawing room last night, which is when she'd first mentioned the task; they'd all been asleep.

Harriet decided to tell them about the task and the deathly threat, about the incident in the bathroom this morning, about the book that mysteriously appeared on her bed and the prisoner called Mohana. Whatever this task was, she figured she couldn't do it alone. Plus, the fact that the others had also seen the woman must've meant that the task involved them too. The idea that she might be an actress seemed less likely. Why would Mum hire someone to do something like that? If she wasn't an actress, then where did she come from?

Wayne paused on hearing what Harriet had to say. "Actually, after that woman said them things, I heard another voice, like a bloke's voice. He said, *Deliver her bones to the Fair by nine. Burn Mohana.*"

"No. That's a Disney film," said Tyrone.

"Mohana, not *Moana*." Wayne rolled his eyes.

Harriet couldn't tell whether Wayne was just humouring her, especially since she'd just mentioned the name *Mohana*. She waited for a blank look or a curl of the lip – nothing. If he was telling the truth, how come he'd heard something different?

Tyrone chewed his lips. "So what happens next then? Where do we even start? None of us know who the woman is, and who's this Silas dude she mentioned?"

Lily shrugged. "The history lady tell us he was the mayor of Hallows Hill during all the witch trials. She said they used to hang women here and sometimes they were burning people at the pole."

A soft smile brought out the dimples in Wayne's cheeks. "Stake."

"That was, like, the seventeenth century," Tyrone added.

Wayne crossed his brows, tossing a ball and catching it. "Maybe he had something to do with the prisoner down the dungeon. You said 1665, right?"

"Oi, do you reckon Mohana was a witch?" Tyrone

gasped. "Makes sense. Mohana was the final prisoner when the witch trials were going on."

"So we are maybe looking for witch's bones?" Lily shuddered.

"Maybe. I think Hallows Hill has something to do with all this too. The history book must've been left on my bed for a reason," said Harriet, the muscles in her chest rigid. The others had turned quiet since she'd mentioned the task. She knew fear when she saw it. "Please. Will you guys help me?"

"Is it just you who's getting killed or is it all of us?" said Tyrone, clicking the muscles in his neck. "If it's just you, then I'm in."

"I honestly don't know," Harriet bit back.

The others exchanged uncertain looks. They couldn't really say no. They'd all seen the same woman, heard her say the same thing. Now they were all just as curious and concerned as each other. Tyrone eventually nodded his head. Lily followed. Wayne muttered a quiet, "Sure." They were soon disturbed when the door flew open. Tyrone yelped in surprise, tumbling backwards to the floor.

A tall, slim woman clip-clopped into the room, dressed in a white blazer and a tight, low-cut black dress that made her bosoms look bigger than beach balls.

Wayne blinked his wide eyes. "Jesus."

Tyrone scrambled to his feet and stood to attention beside Lily and Harriet, not seeming fazed by the beach-ball bosoms at all. Well, that was a first.

The woman blinked her thick, false eyelashes at the four performers standing in stunned silence.

"WHAT ARE YOU ALL STILL DOING HERE? YOUR SHIFTS STARTED FIFTEEN MINUTES AGO. I AM NOT PAYING YOU TO SIT HERE AND CHAT."

"Actually we're standing," Wayne muttered under his breath.

Tyrone gulped. He glanced from the others to Carmela. "Harri wants to ask whether you dreamt about an old woman—"

Lily forced a cough and glared at Tyrone over the rim of her glasses.

Harriet's mum did not look impressed. Her bright red lips screwed into a ball. "IF YOU ARE NOT UP AND OUT OF HERE WITHIN FIVE SECONDS, THEN YOU WILL BE CATCHING THE NEXT TRAIN HOME. DO YOU HEAR ME?"

"Not quite. Can you say it a bit louder?" Wayne squinted his eyes to focus.

Mum shot him the dirtiest look. Ever.

Wayne drummed his belly and eventually saluted in acknowledgement, mooching out of the door wearing a curbed grin, closely followed by Tyrone and Lily. Mum waited until they'd gone before she turned to face Harriet, running a flustered hand over her bronzed skin.

"Hattie, why on earth are you wearing a bedsheet? I realise that you don't like wearing dresses, but you are being paid to be a primrose seller. Your dad really wanted you to get involved in this project. He'd be so disappointed to hear that you couldn't be bothered to make an effort for him."

Was she actually being serious? Since when did she start caring about Dad? Ben took up all her precious time nowadays. And when would she stop calling her Hattie? It annoyed the heck out of her.

"If you actually spoke to Dad instead of shouting at him, then you'd know he was cool with me not working this festival. I'm here because you didn't want to leave me at home practising my photography."

"Don't you dare answer me back, Hattie. All I've ever done is support you, but I won't have you wasting your time playing with that silly OAP camera."

"SLR, Mum," Harriet snapped. Her chest tightened. Mum had no idea about photography. She claimed it was a hobby people did after they retired.

"I'm just trying to help you, but all you do is yell at me at the moment." Mum pulled a compact mirror from her purse and brushed another coat of red lipstick over her already red lips. Snapping her mirror shut, she flicked her eyes to Harriet. "Now. Are you going to the costume store to ask Molly for a clean costume or do you intend to stay in that sheet all day?"

"I didn't have time to see Molly before the briefing. I'm on my way there now." Harriet clenched her teeth.

Mum nodded. "Good. I'll check on you later. I just want to make sure you're OK."

Oh, joy. Harriet made sure she'd walked a safe distance from the weaver's cottage before wiping a hand across her damp eyes. When would Mum stop pretending that she cared about Harriet? She was fake, just like everyone else in Harriet's life.

# SEVEN

# THE FIRST INCIDENT

Harriet took a sluggish walk out of the costume store. She drew in a deep breath and let it rush through her nostrils, cleansing her mind of all things 'mum'. She hoisted up the clean peasant's outfit made for a lady ten times older and twenty times wider than her. It actually looked worse than the bedsheet. Oh well, nothing she could do about it now.

Trying to pass through Shire Square Market was like Christmas Eve at the supermarket. A completely overcrowded nightmare. Over in the corner, a man acting as a doctor dressed in a black cloak, breeches and one of those huge collars that looked like a cat's cone of shame, was standing very sternly behind a table of labelled jars, shoes, fish and other weird things. He was calling guests forward and asking them to guess which seventeenth-century cures they'd recommend for the illnesses that he shouted out. A few yards away, a little boy had been locked in the pillories with a sign around his neck reading 'punished for trimming my granddad's beard on a Sunday'. He giggled nervously as an actor quizzed him in front of the amused audience and his parents, who were filming the whole thing on their phones.

Being a primrose seller didn't involve doing much at all, just wandering around carrying a large basket of primroses on your head and singing, "Two bunches a penny, primroses. Two bunches a penny, primroses!" Oh, and pretending to look interested in silk ribbons. Mum had given Harriet the most boring job on the planet. She'd said she was too young for the photographer role. Too young? What utter rubbish. The guy who'd got the job looked about twelve. Amateur.

And there he was, snapping photos of the jester's show in the centre of Shire Square. Wayne had a massive audience. Most of them were girls, but he still had a bigger audience than the other actors. Dressed in his red and yellow jester outfit, he juggled six red sponge balls into the air, under his legs and behind his back while talking energetically and working the audience to the point you couldn't hear him. You could tell he was a drama student. One of the main reasons Harriet never spoke to him at the training day was because he seemed really actory and loud. What do you say to someone like that? He hadn't exactly made an effort to talk to her either. He'd been too busy being centre of attention.

Oops. He caught her looking. Big mistake. He approached her with an outstretched hand. She nearly forgot to breathe. He was about to involve her in his show, in front of thirty to forty people. She normally hid behind the crowds when an entertainer called for volunteers. Covent Garden was the worst for that. The sensible thing right now would be to pretend she was busy, but the crowd were watching in amused expectation. She had to remind herself that she was a performer. Performers weren't supposed to shy away from crowds, so Mum kept telling her. Begrudgingly, she let him guide her to the middle of his circle, battling to hide the displeasure from her face. Her leg started to tremble. It didn't help when she tripped over the stupid, overlong dress and hurtled towards the ground. Thankfully Wayne grabbed her hand just in time and spun her around like a ballerina, making it appear intentional.

The second he grabbed her hand, a shooting pain zipped from her head into her stomach and she lurched back. Her burning cheeks possibly hinted at her growing embarrassment.

"Style it out," he whispered to her, raising an arm in the air and taking a regal bow.

Acting was definitely not her forte and he knew it. *What the heck is he going to do?* She squirmed inside.

Wayne knelt down on one knee and gazed wistfully up into her eyes, strumming a tune on his musical lute. "*Ah, 'tis thee fair maiden who is said to be wise. Alas, when you meet her, you learn it's all lies.*"

Harriet didn't find it nearly as funny as the audience did. Wayne had just humiliated her in front of all these strangers. It didn't look like he'd finished either. He announced to the audience that Harriet was about to sing and began plucking the tune to 'Lavender's Blue' on his lute before she could stop him. She didn't even have time to feel sick. Lucky she knew the words to the song and used her soft, gentle voice to accompany the music, keeping her eyes focused on her shoes. She was aware that Wayne kept peering up at her with raised eyebrows, nodding his head slowly. She couldn't be sure, but was he impressed? No, surely not. He'd probably heard loads of incredible singers at drama school. She was just, well, a nothing.

"Let's hear it for Miss Primrose Seller!" Wayne gestured towards her at the end of the song and somehow made a slimy wet sponge ball pop out from his mouth, which he placed in Harriet's hands. "Hold that a minute."

Gross. He'd done it on purpose to get a laugh. It worked.

Wayne acknowledged the disgusted look on her face. "Sorry if it's a bit slimy. I had fish guts for breakfast."

Whether he was joking or not, Harriet let the sponge ball drop to the floor, resulting in more laughter from the stupidly annoying audience. By now, he'd started stretching two long, thin modelling balloons, one black and the other green. After he'd blown up the balloons in one breath, he spent several seconds twisting and squeezing them until he'd finished his masterpiece. He presented Harriet with a balloon model of a witch with a green face. The way he'd twisted it made it look uncannily like the old woman they'd seen. Had he done that on purpose?

"Is this what you see when you look in the mirror every morning?" Wayne's eyes sparkled; the edge of his lip curled.

*What a complete and utter arse.* Harriet clenched her jaw.

The audience inhaled an 'ooh' sound, but when they caught Wayne smiling, they began to laugh.

*That's it. I've had enough.* Harriet tightened her fists. Her eyes stung. Her blood boiled hot. *Stop making fun of me. Stop making fun of me.* Mist clouded her eyes. Everything inside her tensed, like it did when she was fuming at Mum. Only this time it felt a million times worse. The urge to pop the balloon and embarrass him in return was growing. *I'll give you fish guts*, she growled. The tension rose inside her, gathering behind her eyes. The pressure built until she couldn't restrain it any longer, and let go.

Wayne stopped to stare at her.

A blast of energy zoomed through her eyes.

*BANG.* The balloon witch in Wayne's hand popped. Something splattered over Wayne's face. It was some kind of pink and red slop that stank of fish. He staggered backwards, eyes wide open, spitting a lump of pink jelly onto the ground. He slumped forwards to retch, to which the audience laughed and clapped, assuming he was taking his bows. He gestured that he'd be taking a quick break and turned to Harriet.

"Are… are you OK? Do you want me to get you some water?" Harriet inched closer to him but stepped back when he waved her away, unable to speak. He'd performed a few magic tricks during his audition; perhaps he was still teasing her and the fish was part of the act.

"What the actual fudge? There weren't nothing in that balloon when I blew it up. Are you messing with me?" Wayne used the palm of his hand to wipe the entrails from his face and waistcoat.

Harriet stared from the fish guts on the floor to Wayne's pale face. "No, of course not. How could I have caused it? You did say that you had fish guts for breakfast. I thought you were playing a joke on me."

"Does it look like I'm playing a joke on you, love?" Wayne grabbed a bottle of water from his rucksack and chucked half of it onto his face. He blinked a spattering of water from his eyes, remaining bent over. "The joke was on me anyway."

"Maybe you deserved it." Oh God. She hadn't meant to say that out loud. It made it sound like she'd caused that to happen, which she hadn't. Just strange and awfully convenient that it happened when it did. What made it even weirder was that she'd imagined fish guts exploding from inside the balloon. She paused. There came that raspy inner voice again, as if in response to her question, *The primrose seller shall prune the tender thorns.*

Prune the tender thorns? That's what the strange woman said last night. She'd forgotten about that part up until now. Did it have a double meaning? Her thoughts immediately ceased when she heard Wayne whistling. In a bid to divert the moment, she took time fumbling around in her satchel for something, anything, avoiding Wayne's stare.

He looked bemused but not angry. "Go on. Don't leave me hanging. What have I done to deserve it?"

She'd have to tell him now. Only, all the anger that she'd felt earlier had disappeared. It didn't help that Wayne was waiting for her to explain herself. "Just… please don't humiliate me in front of an audience again. I don't like being on stage anyway, but you made me look like a complete prat."

"Mate, you do realise that I'm a jester, right? Your mum's paying me to take the piss out of people. It weren't personal, you doughnut." Wayne stretched his lips into a closed smile. His eyes narrowed. "Don't take this the wrong way, but if you don't like performing

– then what are you doing here? You always look fed up, if I'm totally honest."

"So would you be, if your mum kept forcing you to do things you didn't want to do." That came out far more aggressive than she'd intended…

"What, like chucking me out my own house, you mean? Yeah. Point taken." Wayne tossed a stone so that it skidded across the cobbled courtyard.

Harriet caught an unfamiliar anguish flicker behind his eyes. She wanted to ask him what he'd meant about being chucked out, but he didn't seem in the mood to talk about it any further. She decided to change the subject before things got awkward. *Just say anything, Harri, absolutely anything.* "I guess I always look fed up because I have to work with boys who like humiliating me."

"Don't know what you're talking about." Wayne's eyes wandered sideways and he started whistling.

Harriet giggled but quickly screwed her lips to hide her teeth. She hated showing her teeth when she smiled. They weren't straight. "I'm allergic to boys."

"That's unfortunate. Well, you're doing insanely well. You've been chatting to one for the last five minutes and haven't died yet – considering what I smell like right now," said Wayne, his face still pale from the nasty surprise he'd received earlier. "Just wondering, were you wearing orange contacts a minute ago?"

"No, I don't wear contact lenses. Why?" asked Harriet.

"Your eyes… No, never mind. Ignore me." He picked up a fire-eating stick and twirled it in his hand like a majorette baton. "Break's over. I better do some work – unless you've got any more surprises for me?"

"What? That wasn't me. I didn't put fish guts in the balloon!" Harriet heard herself whinge at him. The more she thought about it, the more she began to question herself. She imagined her face was even paler than Wayne's face. Wayne turned back to smile at her, flashing his eyebrows and winking in a flirty way that told her he was just bantering. He did that to all the girls. Still. The most popular boy in Bellsbury just spent over five minutes talking to her.

"Hello, lovely! I see you making big juicy eyes at the jester," Lily cooed, stepping beside Harriet in her long red skirt attached to a grey bodice. Tyrone wasn't far behind her, slipping a pair of pliers into the pocket of his bloodied white apron. They were probably on their short break now. Lily paused on seeing Harriet's expression. "¿Qué pasa, guapa? You look like you are not feeling well?"

Tyrone sniffed the air. "Dude, what's that fish smell? Gross."

"I'm not sure whether you'd believe me," Harriet sighed. She turned just in time to witness Wayne spitting a mouthful of fuel onto a stick, which roared into a plume of fire. Where'd he learn to do all this stuff? It seemed to make all the girls go gaga.

Admittedly, he did look hot – and that wasn't just down to the fire.

He tilted his head back, opened his mouth and began feeding the fire into his mouth.

"Dudes, he's gonna die!" Tyrone panicked, jolting forwards. It might've been the light from the sun, but his green eyes sparkled gold.

Something weird was about to happen. Harriet could just feel it.

# EiGHT

# THE GIFTS REVEALED

And she was right.

The flames stopped dancing and started moving in extreme slow motion – proper *Matrix*-style. Gold embers floated through the air, narrowly missing the stick that had drifted away from Wayne's hand, bobbing in the air above his open mouth. Wayne stared, letting his hand drop to his side. The stick floated in mid-air, slowly gliding downwards.

Up above, a flock of gulls flapped over Tyrone's head, their wings relaxing to such a snail's pace that they drifted through the sky. All the guests moved inch by inch, their heads, their arms, everything. Even their conversations sounded like toys when they run low on batteries. Strangely, none of them seem fazed by it. *Are they even aware they're doing it?* Everyone around them had slowed down – except Harriet and her friends.

Tyrone's eyes switched back to green.

"Bro, seriously. Stop that. You're proper scaring me." Tyrone's panicking went up a notch as he cast wild glances at the scene around him. His quivering hands delved into his apron pockets, his breathing unsteady. Just as he finished his sentence, his eyes flashed gold again.

The floating embers suddenly sped up to normal pace, whizzing around the air like aggressive snowflakes. At the same time, the flock of gulls stopped dawdling and winged their way across the sky, as far from Tyrone as possible. The guest's conversations launched back into a pacey chatter as they applauded the jester for his fire-eating show, oblivious to what had just happened; oblivious to the fact that Wayne never actually finished the show.

Wayne looked directly at Tyrone and held up his hands. "Nothing to do with me. By the way, were you wearing orange contacts too?"

Tyrone fiercely shook his head.

Harriet flinched when that inner voice murmured in her head: *The barber shall learn to shape time itself.* The barber? As in Tyrone? Like what happened just now when everything slowed down? Another sentence spoken by that woman last night.

"Tyrone, how did you do that?" Harriet didn't mean to blurt that out without any explanation. The question had just been an extension of her thoughts.

Tyrone made a weird noise that suggested he'd

asked himself the same question. "Shut up, man. How could I make that happen? I was just standing here. Freaking out, like this—"

"No! Stop! Please don't be doing it anymore." Lily waved her hands at Tyrone. Her brown eyes flashed a fiery gold.

Something weird happened to the tips of her fingers. They glowed like a torch. It reminded Harriet of that alien, ET, when he points his finger to heal people. It must've roasted her fingers because she frantically blew on them as though she'd just applied a fresh coat of nail polish. Trying to cool them down did nothing at all. Instead, from her glowing fingertips, bright gold flames shot out and zoomed into Wayne's burning firestick, which he instantly tossed to the ground. Lily screamed at her hand, flinging it all over the place as if waiting for it to fall off. Her fingertips returned to their normal colour, as did her eyes.

What the heck? Fire had just come out of Lily's fingers. Without using a lighter, a match or rubbing two sticks together. It came from her actual fingers. The audience thought this was part of it. The firestick was still there on the floor. On fire. The flames growing taller, thicker.

"Probably shouldn't just stand here." Wayne was the first out of the four of them to move. He bobbed his head, surveying the courtyard, maybe looking for a bucket of water or hose. When he couldn't find what he wanted, he hurried towards the firestick and lifted his foot directly above the fire.

"No, Wayne. You are crazy!" Lily screeched. She suddenly flinched when her fingertips glowed again, her eyes glittering gold.

This time was different. Instead of fire, pellets of water shot out from all her fingers and showered the fire, and Wayne. It should've been a relief when the fire finally went out and the water stopped flowing, but it only injected more fear into everyone. What they'd seen had definitely happened, right? Lily made fire and water appear from nowhere, using her fingers.

Wayne slowly turned to face Lily, spitting out a jet of water. "Have you finished? What the fudge is up with all your eyes?"

Lily's gold eyes faded to brown and she cupped a hand over her mouth; something she always did to stop herself from crying. She inched towards Wayne but let out a gasp when he inched back. "I am not asking for this to happen to my fingers. I just want it to stop, but I don't know how."

"Easy. Wear boxing gloves," Wayne said matter-of-factly.

Lily didn't take his sarcasm too well. Tears started rolling down her cheeks. "I don't understand why this is happening to me. How can I stop this if I don't know what it is? You don't need to shout at me."

"I'm not shouting at you." Wayne's face softened. He kept his distance from her and paused when she took offence. "Nothing against you, but just don't come anywhere near me. I don't need another bath."

"Try making your fingers light up again. Just once more. It might dry Wayne's clothes." Tyrone sounded confident, but his face had terror written all over it.

Wayne was about to come out with some kind of colourful language, but Lily had already lifted her fingers, staring at them as though she'd never seen them before. Once again, her eyes flicked to gold.

This time, a tornado of wind blasted from Lily's fingers and struck Wayne like a leaf blower, causing his face to flap, dip, wobble and droop in all weird directions. He grabbed his hat, his hair almost taking off, every end poking upright. He couldn't even close his wide-open mouth or talk due to the wind being so strong.

The inner voice rasped again, only this time more familiar: *The dancer will court flames, storm and stream.* When the old woman spoke that sentence last night, she must've been referring to Lily – the same way she'd referred to Harriet and Tyrone…

Wayne's turn next.

Harriet fiddled with her earring. The second she looked at Wayne's costume, she recalled the old woman's words as clear as anything: *The jester shall perform others' wishes.*

The jester was definitely Wayne. Performing wishes? How could he perform a wish? That part didn't make sense. Her heart had never raced so fast.

Harriet decided to try something, without any idea what might happen or whether anything would happen. It was worth a shot. "I wish this would all just stop."

Her attention turned to Wayne, to the waft of smoke rising from both his hands. His ice-blue eyes flashed gold.

In what felt like less than a second, the wind dropped, literally dropped to zero. Wayne's facial features fell back into place. It was like nothing had ever happened.

*

Wayne stumbled back a few steps and threw out his arms to steady himself, his wide ice-blue eyes flicking from left to right.

Lily chewed her lips in the way she did when she was nervous. "¡Madre mía! Harri say for all the wind to stop and it has happened. Do you think… has she made it go away? I am never again using my fingers."

"What, ever? Good luck with life in general," said Wayne.

"Wish. I said the word *wish*. Smoke came out of Wayne's hands." Harriet knew she was mumbling aloud, but she didn't care. Wayne just granted…? No, surely not. His eyes had also changed colour, just like Lily's and Tyrone's had.

"OK. Ever since I met you last night, all this weird stuff has started happening." Wayne's cheerful jester persona had been replaced by something Harriet hadn't seen before. His swollen, bloodshot eyes suggested that maybe he was coming down with a cold.

"Wayne is right. Think about this – we are all having the same dream last night. Since then, I am making different elements from my fingers. Tyrone is slowing down time and Wayne makes wishes come true. All this is happening today. I cannot think of any reason, except magic powers. I know it is sounding crazy, but what else can it be? What is happening to us?" Lily's bushy hair beat against her face. She tugged a chunk of it from her open mouth. "But nothing is happening to you, no?"

Actually something did happen – the balloon incident that Harriet had written off as a coincidence. The more she thought about it, the less likely it seemed like a coincidence, especially after witnessing all the recent incidents. Wayne had also pointed out that her eyes changed colour too. She licked her bottom lip and told Lily and Tyrone exactly what happened. Their silent gasps spoke volumes. Harriet's heart hammered against her chest. She stopped to mull over the words spoken last night.

*Emotion and unity will ignite their strength. Emotion and unity*, she repeated. So did that mean these *powers* were fuelled by their emotions? Thinking about it, they'd all felt something at the time – anger, panic and fear. Could it be the stronger the emotion, the stronger the magic?

She wanted to disagree with Lily about referring to 'it' as magic. Magic was the sort of thing she read about in fiction books or watched in films. It was fantasy, not real life. Then again, magic was the power of influencing events by using mysterious or supernatural forces. There wasn't any point denying it any further. Harriet swallowed hard.

Wayne interrupted Harriet's thoughts by stepping into her personal space. He still had that unfamiliar, un-jester look on his face, his eyes so bloodshot that all the white had practically disappeared. "You found that old gravestone, right? Pretty sure you started all this. Best hurry up and find them bones."

Wow. He blamed her. Maybe he had a point. Was it the weird epitaph on the gravestone that had started all this? If they'd never read the verse from the photo on Harriet's phone, then perhaps they wouldn't have shared the same dream, received an unwelcome visit from a creepy old woman, seen her again this morning – and now magic powers had been thrown into the mix. Magic powers. God, that sounded ludicrous. Harriet realised that she'd inched backwards; being near Wayne kept giving her weird twinges. Ugh, she hated nerves. "Wayne, please. I didn't know this was going to happen."

"OK," said Wayne. The look he shot her was one of accusation.

She opened her mouth, but nothing came out. The twinge in her stomach intensified into a heaving pain and she crumpled forwards, clutching her stomach, her chest. She couldn't stand up straight.

Wayne stopped to stare at her. The others were staring at her too. Not in a 'oh, I can't believe you said that' sort of way. More scared. Actually terrified.

"Harri, what is happening to your face? You look like the lady we see last night. And… and your hair… it's turning black," Lily whimpered.

What the heck was she on about? Harriet grabbed a chunk of her hair and tugged it beneath her nose. A black colour tinged the ends, spiralling its way through every strand. She wanted to scream, but something stopped her. A strange, heaviness inside numbed her muscles. The voice that next came out of her open mouth sounded croaky, inhuman.

"*Magic repulses him. He is among us. Unite, or die…*"

Her voice suddenly rose several octaves and she sang a tune, a tune chanted by the strange woman last night. She couldn't stop herself. "*One little villager hanging from the noose, nobody there to cut them loose… May God have mercy on your soul.*"

No sooner had she finished the sentence than Wayne lunged towards her, his face twisted in fury. His fingers groped her neck as he pinned her against the stony wall behind, slamming her so hard that she cried out. He didn't seem bothered by the panic on her face. His inflamed eyes bore into hers. "I knew it. You're just like her. What else are you hiding?"

"Like who? I'm not hiding anything. Wayne, it's me. Please, stop! You're hurting me," Harriet choked, regaining the strength in her muscles and voice. Copper red streaks fired through the lengths of her hair until all the black disappeared. She gulped several times, staring pleadingly into Wayne's eyes.

As if shaken from a reverie, he let his hands slide from her neck and held them up in surrender. His features softened. The redness faded from his ice-blue eyes. Turning his face away from her, he struggled to compose himself. He snatched the jester hat from his head and returned his eyes to Harriet. "Sorry. I'm sorry."

He didn't give her time to talk. Kicking his shoe against the cobbles, he turned away from his friends and disappeared through Shire Square.

# NiNE

# SPARK OF FRIENDSHIP

The afternoon couldn't have gone slower.

It wasn't easy carrying on as a primrose seller, pretending that nothing had happened when it so obviously had. BIG time. It didn't matter that the black had vanished from her hair as quickly as it'd appeared or that she'd stopped talking and apparently looked like an old woman. The issue was that it even happened. Something, or someone, had gained control of her mind, her speech, her body. Her lips might've been moving, but the words were not her own. How would she have even thought up that stuff?

After it happened, she didn't feel right. Not unwell. Just low. Like all the life had been sucked out of her. Even now, she felt much the same.

Harriet ambled into the castle lounge. The warmth of the roaring fire reminded her of Nan's home, knitting and custard creams. Old books were crammed along the chipped wooden shelves and squared oak tables were set at angles in-between the bookcases, with paper, feather quills and inkpots on each, mainly to keep the kids amused while their parents nattered about the 'shocking' state of the weather. Yes. Cold weather was so unusual for late October.

Only an hour before the next event. Harriet slipped past the piano towards a table at the back of the room and stopped. The back door leading out into the courtyard hung open. Leaning against the wooden frame, Wayne smoked a rolled-up cigarette. She didn't like it that he smoked. It reminded her of the gang who shouted stuff at her on her way home from school, normally relating to her red hair. Two young girls were standing opposite Wayne, listening to something he was saying while messing around with his hair. He didn't look as angry as he had earlier, but he wasn't smiling. Just at that moment, he turned and saw her. *Damn.*

Harriet spun her head the other way. She hadn't forgotten the way he'd hurt her. He blamed her for this mess. What was the betting Lily and Tyrone did too?

Harriet found a spare table hidden behind a polished cabinet stacked with massive leafy plants. It smelt like walking through one of those greenhouses in B&Q, not that she was a frequent visitor. Mum was, though. She had a thing about plants. Harriet couldn't think of anything worse.

Beneath Harriet's hand on the table was a crinkled map of Hallows Hill. Someone clearly had an interest in how Bellsbury used to look. Not much different, apparently. Dad had tried to replicate Hallows Hill as best he could. She glanced down at the map. The Blacksmith's Hut and the Bakehouse were in the same place. Even the old stake and the surrounding Fair hadn't moved. The Washerwoman's Hut hadn't moved either. She leant closer. *What's that red mark next to the Washerwoman's Hut?* For some reason, a small red circle had been etched either on top of or beside the hut. It was difficult to tell. The whole map was so small.

A jester hat clinked on the opposite side of Harriet's table.

She winced and peered up.

Wayne looked back at her, raising the edges of his lips slightly. "You alright?"

"Fine," Harriet replied. She realised how cold she sounded, but she couldn't mask it. She held up the map. "Is this yours?"

Wayne cocked his head to look at it. "Oh, yeah. That. Just found it lying around. I was gonna give it to you. Might be something in it, you never know." He shrugged and drew up a chair, sitting on it so that he was facing her, his hands hanging between his knees. "You got a minute? I need to explain stuff."

"What is there to explain? Earlier, you said this was all my fault. You practically strangled me," Harriet said, the cramping in her stomach sneaking back.

"I know. I didn't mean it. I'm sorry, mate." Wayne looked at her straight in the eye. "I totally get that you're upset with me, but—"

"I'm not upset," Harriet cut in, blinking her eyes at the ceiling.

Wayne raised his eyebrows. "No? Alright then."

"I just didn't expect it, that's all." Harriet tugged at her earlobe. She could still feel his fingers pressing into her neck. "What did you mean when you said that you knew it? You said I'm just like her. You asked me what else I'm hiding."

Wayne looked down at the table for a moment, rubbing his hands over his flustered face. "You know when you think you know someone? I weren't sure who you were. All this weird stuff is freaking me out. You literally threatened us, Harri."

"I didn't. It wasn't me." Harriet bit her lip.

"It's like, every time I trust someone, they mess with my head. I know you were possessed, or whatever weird crap that was; I get it. I'm just… I'm annoyed at my mum, not you."

"I'm sorry." Harriet bowed her head.

Wayne carried on when Harriet's lips trembled. "Don't take it personal. You should probably stay away from me. I'm not a good person. I've got a lot of stuff going on at the moment and I clearly still can't control my temper."

"Oh? What kind of stuff?" Harriet didn't know whether it was her business to ask. She didn't want to stay away from him.

Wayne went quiet for a moment. "Stuff at home. Or what was my home."

If she didn't ask, he wouldn't tell her. She wanted to know more, especially after what he'd said this morning. "Were you really kicked out of your home?"

"Yeah." Wayne sat back and twirled an ace of spades card in-between his fingers. The picture changed to a different playing card each time he flipped it; the last picture looked like a noose, but he shuffled it so quickly it was hard to tell. He looked up at Harriet. "Basically, my mum's a complete joke. I've spent the last nine years looking after my little sister because my mum's too incompetent to do it herself. But did I get any thanks for it? Yeah, right. Don't get me wrong, I'd do anything for my sister, but there weren't no one to look after me."

Harriet fiddled with her earring. "I know this is none of my business, and feel free to tell me to get lost, but why were you kicked out of your home? I don't understand. You just said you had to look after your sister?"

"Yeah, I did. But I'd had enough." Wayne chewed the inside of his cheek and finally spoke again, on seeing Harriet's puzzled expression. "I stayed out every night. Hung around with a bad crowd. Did bad stuff."

"Drugs?" Harriet was already dreading his response.

"That's why Mum kicked me out: 'cos she couldn't deal with me." Wayne deliberately avoided her gaze.

Harriet's heart dropped. She had so many questions, but the fear of asking Wayne the wrong one ruled out most things that were on the tip of her tongue. If Lily were sitting here, she'd be probing him like nobody's business. Maybe she already knew everything. Harriet beamed at Wayne while carefully contemplating her next question. "Thank you for coming over to apologise, by the way."

Wayne raised the edges of his lips into a warm smile.

She loved how his eyes slanted down and crinkled at the edges when he smiled. She'd only just noticed it. Her cheeks flushed as she locked eyes with him and smiled back. For once, she couldn't look away. Neither of them spoke. The intensity was getting too much. She'd lost the ability to string a sentence together.

Wayne's eyes twinkled with wit and he interrupted the silence, his voice softer. "What?"

"Nothing." Harriet's face burned the longer Wayne watched her. She massaged her knotted stomach. What could he possibly be thinking? What did he think about her? She plucked up the guts to ask him her next question. "What about your dad? Didn't he help out?"

"Nope. He buggered off after Izzy was born. He didn't want a deaf daughter with Down's Syndrome. We didn't want a dad with Tosser Syndrome." Wayne looked at Harriet and folded his lips into a closed smile.

"Oh, Wayne. I'm… I don't know what to say," Harriet stuttered.

Wayne shrugged. "You don't have to say anything. I'm over it, mate."

"Your dad sounds like a complete idiot."

Wayne seemed to find her innocence warmly amusing. "That's an understatement, but yeah. I'll go with that."

Harriet shook her head, blinking the disbelief from her eyes. "But where are you living now?"

"Other side of London – Camden. I'm staying at my nan's. She sorted my head out." Wayne's tone became more solemn the more he spoke about his past. The crinkles at the edges of his eyes had vanished.

Harriet wanted to throw her arms around him, but nerves and the uncertainty of not knowing how Wayne would react held her back. She wanted to tell him that her relationship with her mum wasn't much better. He wouldn't be interested in her life. "You're in a better place now, though, right?"

"Sure. Why not?"

"Oh? You look good to me." Harriet scrunched her eyes. That sounded more flirtatious than anything else.

Wayne waggled his eyebrows suggestively. The edge of his lip curled. "Is that right? Thought I'd annoyed you?"

Harriet tossed her hair over her shoulders in an attempt to hide her hot cheeks. She desperately tried to think of a comeback. "You did earlier when you said I looked like a witch."

"That's not what I said." Wayne frowned, then mumbled from the corner of his mouth. "Not in so many words anyway."

Harriet wrinkled her nose. It's like her nerves had evaporated, letting her bask in his presence. She laughed before the words had even left her mouth. "At least I don't wear Eau de Fish Guts."

"Yeah? And whose fault is that?" Wayne smiled crookedly. "So, when were you gonna tell me that you could sing?"

Harriet looked at the table, her heart fluttered. "But I can't."

"Pfft." Wayne scoffed.

Harriet grinned. "My dad thinks I can sing too. I disagree."

Wayne shook his head with a frown. "You're outnumbered on that one. You sounded alright to me. You underestimate yourself." Sighing heavily, he leant forwards. "Listen, I was gonna say, since I got here, there's something…" He stopped. .. rolled downwards, eyebrows knitted. Two strea .. red leaked from his nose and ran down his lips. He sniffed twice and smeared a hand across his nose, breathing through his mouth.

"Wayne, are you OK?" Harriet delved into her right pocket and whipped out a wad of crinkled tissues. She waited for him to dab the red blobs from beneath his freckled nose. "What were you about to say?"

Wayne wiped another streak of red dribbling down his lips, swearing to himself when it trickled onto his waistcoat. A glint of torment passed over his eyes, almost like he wanted to tell her something. He tossed a playing card in the air and caught it again, rising to his feet. "Don't matter. Weren't important. Anyway, gotta go. Catch you later, love."

*He's lying*, were the words she heard in her head. Wayne hadn't told her everything, but then why would he? His life was none of her business. When he left through the main doors, the voice croaked again, repeating what had been circling her head all morning: *Bury the bones, together, before the ninth hour on Halloween night. Betrayal is upon you.*

## TEN

# THE BANQUET

"I really don't want to be here tonight." Harriet huddled by the roasting fireplace, breathing through her mouth to block out the waft of roast meats and crusty pies. Missing dinner earlier couldn't have been a worse idea.

Two long benches ran parallel to the side stone walls where around one hundred other guests sat, downing goblets of ale. Dad's favourite drink. Gross. Looked like wee.

Tyrone scowled when an inebriated man slurred, "Wassail!" in his earhole. You could just about see him under the broad-brimmed hat with a feather poking out. He tossed a mane of loose brown curls over his shoulder like a model from a shampoo advert. "By the way, I text my mum about what happened today. I thought she might be able to diagnose our weird condition – but she told me to grow up and stop mucking about. She's a nurse; she's supposed to know everything, man. Well annoyed."

"Tyrone, nurses are only trained to deal with medical issues, not weird magical powers. Of course your mum's not going to believe you," said Harriet. Why had he even told his mum in the first place? Nobody would believe him. She was struggling to believe it.

Tyrone folded his arms. "Whatever. You're stressing, aren't you? You reckon something might happen tonight."

Harriet's insides twisted into a tight knot. Unexplained incidents had happened throughout the whole day like with the balloon, the slowing down of time and the sudden hurricane. What's to say the weirdness would stop now?

Biting her lip, Harriet gazed around the bustling banquet hall. When was a good time to test the idea that they really had magic powers? When this festival was over? Her insides clenched up. It was like getting a new phone and not being able to use it for one whole evening.

Lily looked as beautiful as ever, but underneath those dark curls and immaculately applied make-up she struggled to hide the trauma of today. She might've been twirling and swaying like a country dancer in the centre of the hall with the other dancers, but those who knew her could see that she didn't want to be here either.

The guests started banging their fists against the table and stomping their feet. Anyone would've thought they were being impatient when actually they were applauding the jester, Wayne, who'd just performed a load of backflips, cartwheels and handstands while juggling apples and prancing around beside Lily, parodying her dance. Unlike Lily, he'd been trained to act, to mask any troubles underneath his façade.

"Oi, ginge, go get me some water!" Jazz shouted over the noise. "Bet you thought you were right in there earlier when Wayne was chatting to you. He's so out of your league, you know that, right?"

So had Wayne slagged off Harriet to Jazz, after he'd spoken to her this afternoon? Maybe he wasn't so genuine after all.

"Tell you what though, he's good in bed." Jazz smirked. She laughed at something on her phone. She didn't hesitate to shove the screen in Harriet's face, baring a snarl dripping with satisfaction. "Look what Ellie just text me. She had a massive house party the other Saturday and invited us all after the training day. Everybody was so wild that night… oh, did you not get invited? Shame. I thought that Lily might've told you."

"I…" Harriet stammered. She never knew how to respond to Jazz's insults.

Tonight must've been Jazz's free shift. So why wouldn't she choose to spend it here, intent on making Harriet's job a complete nightmare? She grinned when Wayne bounded onto the bench before her, talking dynamically. Harriet inched backwards and bit her lip, staring at a blank spot on the wall, pretending that it didn't bother her. Jazz's eyes crept in Harriet's direction and she moved closer to Wayne, wrapping her arms around his neck. He hugged her back, massaging her hair. For a minute, it looked like they were kissing. Harriet looked away again. Tears welled up in her eyes. A heavy weight pressed down on her chest.

There came that weird feeling again. Harriet's eyes began to tingle. Her blood heated up, eyes turned foggy. *Why can't you just shrivel up and die?* she grumbled. The elegant mirror hanging on the opposite wall reflected her dazzling gold eyes.

Oh God.

Jazz was still cuddling and laughing at Wayne, but it sounded different. More like a dying croak. The near-to-empty glass she'd been holding slipped from her fingers, smashing to the cold floor. Wet drops dribbled around her twitching shoes.

"Look at her fingers," a short man on her bench uttered. "Her fingers – they're getting thinner."

He was right. A minute ago, Jazz had full, perfectly manicured fingers. Now, they looked more like twiglets, skinny and long. She raised a skeletal hand to scratch her head. Clumps of white hair came away in her fingers and floated to the ground. Wrinkles dipped into her heart-shaped face, her hands and her legs, making her look fifty times older. Within a couple of seconds, her body shrank so much that her jeans dropped to her ankles. Bones started protruding through her tissue-like skin.

"Help, what's happening to me?" she squawked, grabbing onto the bench. One after the other, her teeth dropped out. "Wayne, help me!"

Wayne's face twisted in horror and he swore silently. His eyes flicked to Harriet. "Swear to me this wasn't you."

Harriet opened her mouth. She couldn't speak.

"Jazz, what... what's happening to you? Someone, please help! Call a first aider," Harriet heard a girl shout. What would you say to a first aider? This wasn't exactly a first aid case. It was a... supernatural case.

Almost half the bench flocked around Jazz. Some people yelled at her for playing a sick joke. Others screamed, unable to look at the decomposing mess she'd become. Soon, all that was left were a pair of slim blue jeans, a red velvet top, purple underwear and a pair of high-heeled boots. The bones of a human skeleton poked out from every hole in her clothing.

*

The friends herded the guests and staff out of the hall, announcing that under Carmela's direction the banquet was over, while assuring them that what happened to Jazz was a Halloween trick. Harriet swallowed several times. An unbearable ache swelled in the pit of her stomach. She'd caused this. She'd actually caused this. What more proof did she need? She had magic powers. Did that make her a witch? *Witch*, she said to herself. *Witch. I'm a witch. I. Am. A. Witch.* The more she said it, the more outrageous and weird it sounded. She had to put this right again. Surely it was just a case of enforcing the thought of Jazz turning back to normal in her mind.

It didn't matter how many times she repeated, *Turn Jazz back to normal*, in as many different ways she could think of – nothing happened. Earlier she'd concluded that the magic was fuelled by emotion. It didn't take a genius to figure out that she didn't feel much for Jazz at all. However, Wayne obviously did. He was her next and only hope. This had to work. Harriet closed her eyes, clutching her trembling fingers. *I wish for Jazz to turn back to normal, right now*, she pleaded.

She waited a couple of seconds before forcing open her eyes. Wayne flicked his gold eyes back at her with a faint smile and nodded towards the corner.

The decomposing mess of bones and clothing had disappeared from the floor. Jazz was now slumped in her chair, fully dressed, head bowed forwards. Her eyes were shut.

"Is… is she alive?" Harriet stammered.

Tyrone crept across to Jazz, being cautious not to disturb her in case she might jump out at him. He peered into her face and waved his hand past her closed eyes. Nothing. Shaking his head at Harriet, he gently lifted Jazz's wrist to feel her pulse. It must've been something his mum had taught him to do, being a nurse. His shoulders relaxed. "She's breathing. She's fine. I reckon she just needs rest or something. Doubt she'll remember this, though. All the guests were totally oblivious to our magic this morning."

Harriet nodded silently. Wayne had just fixed her mess and he knew it. He'd just chosen not to say anything about it. At least that was one less thing to worry about and she wouldn't go down for murder. Not that she would. Technically, she never laid a finger on Jazz. It hadn't stopped her heart from pounding as she'd hoped. In fact, it sped up to the point that she felt breathless.

A tense calm filled the hall.

Then a deep voice bellowed out, "*He has possessed the innocent.*" It was so loud, Harriet couldn't tell whether it had come from nearby or was in her own mind. It wasn't the usual inner voice she'd been hearing. She threw fleeting glances around her, at the table laden with half-eaten chicken and spilt drinks, the rat scurrying out from beneath the chair in the corner, Wayne staring at the wall, rubbing a hand against his bloodshot eyes, and Lily and Tyrone staring at Jazz, who remained in a coma. "*You have* revived Mohana's spirit and her magic," the voice hissed. "Deliver her bones to the Fair by nine o'clock to put an end to this curse."

Harriet staggered backwards, throwing glances around the hall. This was serious. If she didn't bury the bones before nine on Halloween night, would she die like she was warned in the dream?

"Did you hear that voice just now?" Harriet stared at the others. Judging by Tyrone and Lily's expression, she gathered they'd not heard anything. Wayne's face, however, was impassive. "It said, *You have revived Mohana's spirit and her magic.*"

"Mohana? Isn't that the final prisoner you read about in the book? She's the witch whose bones we need, right?" Tyrone's voice echoed through the hall.

"Actually, Wayne, didn't you say you heard the name Mohana instead of Silas in your dream? That she's returned?" Harriet asked him.

"Mohana?" Wayne pursed his lips and considered her question. He shook his head. "No. Never heard of her."

Harriet was sure he'd said it. Tyrone had even joked about the film *Moana* in response. She decided not to question him any further just in case he lost his temper with her again. She switched her attention to Tyrone instead. "Tyrone, while you've got your phone out, could you Google Mohana? Maybe type in Hallows Hill too. I'm just curious about who this woman really is."

Tyrone jumped on it straight away.

Nobody spoke. Nobody breathed. They waited.

Something caused his eyes to widen, his brows drawing together. He swallowed several times, hands trembling.

"…Tyrone?" Lily braced herself for his response.

Wayne's eyes remained on Tyrone.

"No way… Dudes, she's dead," Tyrone stammered.

There must have been more to it than that. Harriet moved closer to him. "We know that, Tyrone, but—"

Tyrone raised his voice. "Just listen, yeah? Mohana Oakes is… she… look, check out this picture for yourself." Tyrone turned his phone to face the others, hand still shaking.

It was a sketch of a woman. She looked to be in her late fifties, early sixties. Her bushy black hair fell below the shoulder line of her long-faded black dress. She hung from a noose attached to what looked like the gallows. Her head was tilted to one side, hands tied together, eyes shut. Below the image was the text *Mohana Oakes, hanged on 31st October 1665.*

No… it couldn't be. Oh God.

"Mohana Oakes is the lady in black," Harriet gasped. She wanted to throw up. She'd seen a ghost, not an actress. Did that mean the voices she'd heard recently belonged to Mohana? It would make sense.

"I'm proper bricking it now, man. We need to find her bones. It's Halloween tomorrow night and I don't wanna die," Tyrone stressed.

Lily took a shuddering breath. "Yes, I agree. We probably will only be out for a couple of hours."

"Not if her bones are in Australia you won't," said Wayne.

"Don't make jokes," Lily whinged at him. "But where we are burying the bones?"

Harriet replayed the words in her head. "That's the thing. Mohana keeps telling me to bury the bones, but then that other voice said to *deliver her bones* to the Fair."

"The Fair? Why the Fair? That is not a normal place to bury bones," said Lily, chewing the ends of her hair. "You should listen to Mohana. The other voice might be Silas, no?"

Tyrone stepped closer to Harriet. "Do you reckon that this Silas geezer is going to be the one to kill us?"

Harriet nodded. "I think his spirit has come back and possessed someone in this village. That's how that voice just made it sound. Someone we know is going to betray us."

Wayne stifled a smirk, focusing on the ground.

"Don't insult me," Harriet barked at him, to which he raised his hands. She wasn't being ridiculous. She wasn't… was she? Her eyes landed on Jazz. Could she be possessed by Silas? She behaved like an evil monster half the time. Maybe Jazz wasn't really in a coma and was eavesdropping on their conversation. It would explain why Jazz hated Harriet so much.

Panic rang in Lily's eyes, her eyebrows crossed. "So Silas wants to get rid of us because we all have Mohana's magic. I don't know why nine o'clock and I don't know why Silas hates Mohana so much, but we need to find and bury her bones before he can find us."

"I think he already has," Harriet whispered.

# ELEVEN

# THE COFFEE HOUSE PLOT

Today was Halloween. Harriet hadn't slept one bit. Too many thoughts and questions had been hurtling around her mind, her heartbeat pulsing through her head. There wasn't any doubt that Harriet suffered from anxiety, but this was more than that. It was terror. Terror of not knowing how today would end. Terror of what would happen if she couldn't locate the bones.

She'd dreamt about the girl in the thick hooded coat hanging from a noose again. It definitely didn't look like Mohana; this girl seemed young. If it wasn't Mohana, then who was it? If only she could rewind back to a couple of nights ago and undo every incident that took place that night – starting with her accidental fumble with the grave. She wouldn't be in this situation now.

*What's done is done*, Dad would say.

Harriet arrived at the Coffee House around one o'clock to meet the others, who were already there waiting for her. It was the quickest they could escape from their jobs to meet up with one another without anyone noticing. She hurried through the great wooden hall decorated with chandeliers, rows of long wooden tables and large glass windows. She was surrounded by a mixed group of merchants, traders, wizards, witches and poets dressed in doublets and curly wigs. Over in the corner, a young guy pretended to smoke a long clay pipe while reading *The Bellsbury Gazette* by the fireplace.

Harriet dodged the labyrinth of tables and found Lily, Wayne and Tyrone sat in silence at a table behind a young couple. Lily sipped her coffee, eyes darting all over the place. Tyrone tapped his foot, drumming his fingers on the screen of his phone. Wayne was slumped forwards in his seat, chin resting on his elbows, looking out of the window. He looked different when he wasn't dressed as a jester. Scruffy, but cool. He wore a light green hoodie over a tight white T-shirt, grey beanie hat and faded ripped denim jeans. He half-heartedly saluted at her as she sat down beside Lily.

"Hey," she greeted her friends. The response she received was minimal, more like a collective mutter. Jazz had probably been on their minds.

Last night, they'd decided to leave Jazz asleep in the hall in hope that she'd wake up in the middle of the night and head back to her room, completely unaware about what happened. The fact that she was breathing proved she'd be OK. Harriet hadn't yet seen her in the village. Bet she was psyching herself up to become Silas.

Harriet rubbed her face. She still had the horrible notion that the others blamed her for all this. In truth, she'd started it; no question about that. It just hurt to think that her friends were probably talking behind her back. Did they even care what she thought? She could only wish. Oh, take that back. Damn.

A screwed-up serviette whacked her forehead. She peered up. Wayne looked across the table at her and blew a long raspberry. At least the wish was too vague for him to grant. But it would appear that he'd heard it. "You OK?"

Harriet nodded, trying to hide her embarrassment.

Wayne's smile was as half-hearted as his salute, but he gave her one of his flirty winks. OK, so he might've been a confident, loud performer, but she really liked him, despite all the nervous pains he was unintentionally causing her.

Lily gently cupped Harriet's hands. "Harri, how are we finding these bones? The hours are counting down."

"Didn't Mohana hint at where she was buried in the dream? I'm sure she said something about her location," said Harriet. She now regretted not writing down every word when it'd been fresh in her mind yesterday.

"Yeah, she said she's in a cage where bugs eat flesh or something," said Tyrone.

Wayne furrowed his brows. "Where is she, in a zoo?"

A cage. An iron cage! Of course. There was that article about it yesterday morning. She'd kick herself in a minute if she couldn't remember what she'd read in that history book. She closed her eyes. Words filtered into her mind in dribs and drabs: secret passageways, a lost dungeon beneath the prison. She growled out loud, causing Lily to jump. "Sorry. I'm just trying to remember what I read in the history book, the one that was left on my bed."

"I already tell you that I didn't leave it on your bed," said Lily, seeming quite agitated. And who could blame her.

"I know you didn't. I've figured that Mohana deliberately left it on my bed as a clue to her location," said Harriet, scrunching her damp fingers together.

"Mohana? Are you actually joking? How can she leave a book on your bed? She's dead," Tyrone scoffed at her.

"I'm being serious. She bookmarked it to the page about Hallows Hill prison and dungeons for us to find. It was a clue to her location. It said the body of the last prisoner has been in a cage since Halloween 1665."

"Nearly four hundred years ago today," said Wayne. He sat back in his chair. "Do you reckon she might've come in here for a cream tea before her death?"

Tyrone's chuckle turned into a high-pitched whimper.

Harriet rewound back to last night at the banquet. "That black and white photo showed that she was hanged on the gallows. She looked like that when I saw her in the drawing room. So after her execution, her body must've been locked in the dungeon to rot."

"So what's her gravestone for then?" Wayne knitted his brows.

Harriet recalled Mohana's crumbly gravestone among all the other posh ones, and how out of place it'd looked, especially without the date and name. Only the hand carving had made it appear authentic. Perhaps the idea had been stolen from the gravestone with the carved man's hand? Now it made sense. It wasn't a real gravestone. "It was put there to bring her back – and we have. It wasn't a glow-up gravestone. She'd cursed it with her spell."

It was all starting to fall into place now. Surely this was it. Once they'd found out exactly where the bones were hidden, then they could complete their task and the curse would be lifted. A sudden bout of faith made her feel ten times lighter. "I guess we just head into the prison and her bones will be inside."

"Yes, but she say her bones are under our feet. The prison is above ground. I think we are getting warm, but not hot yet," said Lily, referring to a game that Harriet taught her how to play when they'd hidden each other's Easter eggs.

Wait. Mohana's death date – 31st October 1665; written numerically that would be 311065. Harriet's heart stopped. She delved into her satchel and grabbed the key that she'd found in the graveyard the night before, holding it up to her face. Just as she thought, there it was, engraved on the bow of the key, Mohana's death date. And those letters above the date: HHD. *HHD?* What did that mean?

There was that section in the book about archaeologists finding secret passageways below the jail yard some hundred years ago. Lily was right. How on earth were they going to get underneath the prison? There weren't any subways or underground tunnels around there. The only other buildings down Olde Pie Streete were an old tavern and the Washerwoman's Hut.

It surprised her how quickly she remembered that. There were so many shops and huts in the village. It was impossible to know where everything was located. Actually, that map she found in the castle lounge had pinpointed the Washerwoman's Hut. In fact, it'd been marked with a red circle.

That same bout of faith washed over her and she let out a breath. She slipped a hand into her other pocket. Her fingers grazed against a folded square of paper. If a heart could actually skip a beat, then hers skipped several beats. This had to be the final piece to the puzzle. She pinched the paper from her pocket and unfolded the crinkled map.

"Wayne found this map earlier and thought it might come in handy. I think he might be right." Harriet held up the map as though she were hosting a presentation to the class. "Look at where the Washerwoman's Hut is – someone's drawn a red circle beside it."

Tyrone leant over to get a closer look. "And?"

"And I think it was deliberately left for us to find in the castle lounge. Someone's helping us find the bones…"

"Let me guess? Mohana?" Tyrone's voice dripped with doubt. "Dude, ghosts don't leave maps and books for people to find."

"Well, someone's helping us. The Washerwoman's Hut is basically opposite the prison. The red circle isn't on the hut itself, but just beside it," said Harriet; her voice had become a whisper. People on other tables were starting to look over.

"You are saying that the bones are buried in the Washerwoman's Hut?" Lily chewed the ends of her hair.

"No. I'm saying that there must be something just outside the Washerwoman's Hut that could be linked to the prison – like the entry to the secret dungeon, perhaps? I think we should go and investigate," Harriet urged.

Wayne scrunched his lips and watched Harriet in question. "When?"

"Now." Harriet kept her eyes on the table, aware that the others were now staring at her in a poised silence. They didn't seem so eager now. When were they expecting to go? Tomorrow, after all this was over? By which time, they'd be dead. Didn't they understand the severity of the situation? What would it take to make them realise that their lives were in danger?

"You for real?" said Tyrone, bouncing his fist against the table.

"Do I look like I'm joking?" said Harriet, her temper running thin. She'd never been a violent person, but she felt the need to punch something. "If we don't find Mohana's bones by nine o'clock tonight, then we will die. Is that what you want?"

Lily tipped her glasses up with a shaky finger. "No, but we should get right all our facts before doing anything."

"We don't have time. What part of this task don't you get?" Harriet growled. Deep down, she knew it wasn't that her friends couldn't be bothered. They were scared. By putting off going to investigate, it meant turning a blind eye to the inevitable. It'd started; her eyes began to simmer. She stared at the empty cup sitting in front of her. A crack zigzagged its way down the middle of the cup, causing the porcelain to split into hundreds of tiny fragments. A small heap tinkled to the hard floor. The loud burst sent Harriet's hands flying to her face. Trying to manage their powers – emotions – was going to be challenging. Most of the time, emotions were unpredictable.

A mutual exchange of looks crossed between Harriet and her friends.

Without saying a single word, Lily, Wayne and Tyrone stood up from their seats, slipped into their jackets, and waited for Harriet to lead them out of the Coffee House and towards the Washerwoman's Hut.

# TWELVE

# TUNNEL TO THE UNDERGROUND

Everywhere bustled with Halloween activity. Harriet and her friends trooped out of the Coffee House and continued down Goulding Lane. A long queue of costumed kids and their non-costumed parents had formed outside the Potions Lab. A waft of purple and green smoke spiralled out of the doorway where a girl dressed as a witch granted them entry in the creepiest voice she could muster. When she spied Wayne, she fluttered her fingers at him in a stupid, gooey way, completely ruining her eerie persona. He nodded back at her in acknowledgment.

Tyrone mooched backwards to join Harriet, leaving Lily and Wayne in front. He remained in silence for a minute or so and took one look at her then threw a glance at Wayne. "You like him, don't you?"

"He's a friend, yeah." Harriet couldn't look up. Seeing Lily and Wayne laugh together felt like a kick in the stomach. "He likes Lily anyway."

"True." Tyrone leaped over a pile of spilled rubbish, holding out his hands to steady himself. "But he doesn't like her in that way, though, I can tell. Wayne gets on with everyone, man."

"Really?" Harriet's insides dissolved into gloop. "Does he… has he ever said anything bad about me?"

"You? Nah, why would he? I know he's got stuff going on and that, but he's solid. He's got your back." Tyrone scuffed his trainer on the pavement.

Harriet beamed on the inside. She would've given Tyrone a hug if he was the affectionate type. Funny that his mum was a nurse who showed her patients affection on a daily basis, yet her son treated people like they all had Chickenpox.

The time on the church clock had just gone half past three. Five and a half hours left. A lump of sick inched up her throat.

So many more questions whizzed around her head. All the kids were dashing about enjoying the Halloween festivities. How would Silas get rid of them? What did it mean to become part of the curse? Would she continue as a spirit, reliving her death every Halloween like Mohana? She couldn't think about it anymore.

She hadn't even realised that they were walking along Olde Pie Streete. She'd been so wrapped up in her own thoughts that she'd lost all awareness of what was going on around her, including a boy who had to swerve around her. That woke her up.

Lily's face appeared over her shoulder. "We are here. Where is the map?"

The hut stood directly in front of them: a small beamed cottage with a thatched roof bigger than the building itself. A tiny oak table sat outside the open door where upon it was a brown bucket filled with water. A long line of laundry was attached from the roof to a nearby signpost. Wayne and Tyrone were already wandering around outside the hut, inspecting the area.

"What are we supposed to be looking for?" said Wayne, jerking back as a large pair of pink knickers hit him in the face. "Bloody hell. Who hung their tent out to dry?"

Tyrone snorted like a pig, elbowing Wayne in the chest.

Lily threw glances everywhere and spoke quietly. "What did that book say, Harri?"

Harriet focused her attention back on the red circle on the map, recalling the passage from the history book. "Archaeologists. Oh, yes. It said they found a way to the secret dungeon by removing iron covers."

"Iron covers?" Wayne and Tyrone mouthed back in question.

"There is only the cobbles here," said Lily.

Harriet stared hard at the map. Although the red circled area was definitely outside the hut, it was still vague. They were all roughly standing in the pinpointed spot and couldn't see anything that resembled any sort of iron cover. Maybe she'd got it wrong and it wasn't a clue after all.

"Are we even in the right place? Look, it's getting proper busy," said Tyrone, pointing to the growing number of guests queuing outside the Ghost Walk booking booth further at the end of the street.

"What do you expect? It's Halloween, darlin'," said the chirpy voice of an older woman. She nudged Wayne, while scrutinising the ground. "What've you all lost? I've got good eyesight, you know. Or is it me you're looking for?"

Harriet gasped. Where on earth had Lottie the washerwoman come from? Again, she'd been too busy searching to notice her. How long had she been standing there? She must've just come back from her lunch break to find them all acting dodgy outside her hut. What hurried response could Harriet possibly give without looking suspicious? Instead, she decided to remain silent, hoping that somebody else would answer.

"Uh… this," Tyrone blurted out. He bent down and picked up the nearest object in his line of vision and flourished it in the air. "A dead snail. Wayne collects them, you see. Uh, here you go, Wayne."

*For goodness' sake, Tyrone.* Harriet crumpled her face.

"Ew." Lottie pulled a face. "Is this a regular hobby of yours, darlin'?"

Wayne's face dropped. He didn't really need to say anything. His face said it all. He remained in a daze as Tyrone dropped the dead snail into his open hand. "Apparently so. Couldn't think of a better way to spend my time."

Lily started giggling and covered her mouth.

"Oh, my. That's quite a weird thing to do," said Lottie, cupping her hands on her face. "What are you going to do with it then, darlin'?"

Wayne muttered something under his breath that sounded like 'muck knows', but then fixed a wide smile and said out loud. "Put it in a box with all the other ones."

Harriet flicked her eyes to Lottie. The poor woman couldn't figure out whether he was joking. She didn't know him well enough to recognise his no-blinking thing. Only problem was, she wasn't going anywhere. She'd seen that they'd found what they were looking for, so what reason did they have to stick around? For a few moments, they all stood there exchanging awkward glances, waiting for the other to make some kind of move.

Harriet focused her gaze back to the ground. Not because she couldn't think of anything to say, but because her eyes had locked on to a section of ground outside the hut. She paused. Something brown and rusty caught her eye on the cobbled street. "What's that you're standing on, Wayne? There, just under your feet."

Wayne looked down and sidestepped to the right.

Just outside the hut, on the ground, was a large rectangular panel, like those manhole covers in pavements. It looked like it hadn't been touched in years. This had to be it. It was more or less where the red circle had indicated.

Wayne, Lily and Tyrone looked from the rectangular panel and back to Harriet. They nodded their understanding, eyes sidling to Lottie. They had to do something about her first.

"I just *wish* she'd go away," Harriet murmured, praying that this would work, praying that his emotions were strong enough to grant the wish.

Wayne's eyes crept to Harriet and he raised his eyebrows in question. "Yeah. Bit vague, mate. Where?"

"I don't know. Anywhere." Harriet spoke without making her lips move, forcing a smile when Lottie looked at her.

Wayne responded with a facial shrug. Gold flared in his eyes. He let the smoke rise from his hands. It enveloped Lottie in a huge, hazy cloud. Her loud coughing and spluttering grew fainter as the smoke gradually faded to nothing.

Lottie was nowhere to be seen.

Harriet picked at her teeth, casting glimpses everywhere. "Wh… where did you send her?"

"Zimbabwe," Wayne replied nonchalantly. He made big eyes at Harriet's expression. "What? You said anywhere."

"Wayne! I just assumed you'd pick somewhere in this village, not another country," Harriet exclaimed.

"Am I also psychic now?" said Wayne, giving her a tight-lipped smile. "Chill out, *darlin'*. She'll be alright. I hear the beach is immense."

Lily jumped in at that point. "Forget Lottie for now, it is quarter past four! It's starting to get dark."

Harriet stuffed the map back in her pocket and stared at the iron cover. In the left-hand corner, three large letters were inscribed into the iron. She didn't have to move any closer to see that the letters read HHD. A spark ignited in her head. Tyrone's silly interpretation, '*Harriet's Hair Disaster*', popped into her head. He'd been talking about the letters on the key. Hastily, she grabbed the key in her pocket and studied the letters on the bow again. HHD. It seemed so obvious now. *Hallows Hill Dungeon.* Mohana was definitely down here. Only the iron cover didn't have a keyhole, which meant the key only opened Mohana's cage. Harriet slipped the key back into her pocket. "OK. I think we'll have to use magic. I can't see how else we're going to open this cover without any tools. Unless you guys have any better ideas?"

Tyrone shook his head. Wayne shrugged. Lily bowed her head.

"OK. Wayne, I wish for the iron cover to open," said Harriet, closing her eyes. She wasn't sure where she'd developed that habit from. It just felt right to shut her eyes when making a wish, like it'd be more likely to come true.

Wayne's face twisted and strained as though he was struggling to concentrate. There wasn't any smoke. His eyes remained ice-blue. The iron cover remained shut. He hung his head and sighed. "I'm not feeling it. I'm sorry. It ain't happening for me."

Harriet nodded. None of his emotions were strong enough at the moment, which meant he wasn't feeling much at all. That came as a surprise considering the critical situation they were in right now. He should at least be feeling scared or anxious or frustrated. Perhaps the last wish drained him of his energy. She guessed it was down to her to open the iron cover with her own magic. Deep down, she hadn't a clue what their next step would be when she did manage to open it. She was better at pretending than she thought.

"Here goes," Harriet uttered. She stared at the iron cover. *I need you to open right now. I'm imagining my fingers undoing the bolts and lifting the panel from the ground*, she repeated to the iron rectangle. A sudden heat shot through her eyes and she clenched her fists into tight balls. Her whole body trembled like a volcano about to erupt.

"Dude, some guests are walking this way. They must think this is a demonstration or something," Tyrone panicked. Without even thinking or meaning to, his eyes blazed gold and he somehow managed to slow their movements right down so that they practically froze. "Come on, man. Hurry up. They're gonna go back to normal in a minute."

*Open right now, open right now. Come on, come on*, Harriet chanted, her eyes scorching to the point of pain, fear creeping up inside her.

From beneath the iron cover something twisted and creaked, like screws being loosened. The whole cover clunked. A gap appeared between the cover and the ground. It worked! Harriet blinked the water from her eyes and let out a breath. They'd have to do this as quickly as possible while Tyrone delayed the guests. Beads of sweat were forming on his forehead. Using these powers wasn't easy. It could only be described like a strenuous PE lesson that left you gasping for breath by the end.

"Can one of you give me a hand?" said Wayne, clutching one end of the panel.

Of course, Tyrone wasn't able to help. His mind was focused on keeping those guests at bay. Harriet quickly grabbed the other end of the iron cover and helped Wayne lift it from the rectangular gap on the ground, nodding when he gave her careful instructions where to move it, all the time checking she was OK. They placed it carefully on the ground.

Harriet peered over the edge of the rectangular gap. She couldn't see anything but blackness. All of a sudden she couldn't breathe. How on earth would this work? They might fall and break their necks.

It was almost like Wayne could read her thoughts. He perched on the edge of the gap and swung his legs about. His trainer whacked against something hard and metallic that echoed down the black tunnel. Flashing his eyebrows at the others, he rolled onto his front and inched down into the black hole. "You'll be fine. There's a ladder here. Dunno how Lily will cope with all the spiders, though. I say we leave her here."

Lily squealed, to which Wayne gave her a fixed dimpled smile.

His face lowered beneath the entrance to the tunnel, followed by the top of his blond head. He'd gone.

"Seriously, you'll both have to speed it up. I can't hold this lot back anymore," said Tyrone, rubbing a clammy hand across his shaved head. His eyes returned to green.

The guests jolted forwards, their movements speeding back up to normal. Just like nothing had ever happened, they carried on heading in the direction of the Washerwoman's Hut.

Taking a faltering breath, Harriet inched down into the tunnel. The cobbles, the approaching feet and the light grey clouds suddenly vanished into an abyss of black nothingness.

# THIRTEEN

# THE SECRET DUNGEON

Being the last to enter, Tyrone hauled the panel back over the gap, leaving a small enough opening for a beam of light to stream through. Large chunks of brick and rubble tumbled down the corroding tunnel walls and eventually splashed to the bottom.

One behind the other, they clanked down the rickety ladder, listening to the sounds of soil scattering onto the ladder rungs and drops of water tapping onto a surface. Harriet tread cautiously. She had visions of this whole ladder falling apart. Every time she grabbed a rung, shreds of eroded metal peeled away in her hands. It made her question whether those archaeologists ever actually made it this far, or had they just found the iron panel on the ground? Harriet bit her tongue. What the heck was she doing? She glanced back up at the panel. What if they couldn't get back out to bury these bones at nine o'clock? What if Jazz was down there waiting for them?

*You are on the right track, keep going,* her inner voice persisted. That should've been reassuring, but instead it planted more fear inside her. It was the unexpected, the not knowing what she'd find at the bottom. A colony of snakes writhed around her stomach and spiralled up her throat. She choked on her own spit.

Wayne stopped to look up at her. "If you're gonna vom, let me pull my hood up first."

"I'm fine," Harriet lied, swallowing the spit that'd gathered in her mouth. She nearly choked again when Lily's small heel landed on her fingers. Yanking her hand away, she bellowed in pain. "Lily! You just stood on my hand. Watch where you're putting your feet."

"I'm sorry, but I can't see anything. My glasses are all the time steaming up," Lily whined.

Tyrone let out a loud yelp. "Man, there are, like, actual leeches in here. We use pretend ones at the barber surgeons. Apparently they love it if you've had a limb amputated."

Wayne continued down the ladder. "So, at your barber surgeons, do you offer customers a cup of tea while you're chopping off their leg?"

Lily raised her voice over Tyrone's nervous snigger. "Wayne! *¿Estamos cerca?*"

"Eh?" Wayne shouted back from below.

"Oh, sorry. I am nervous. I say, are we close?" Lily squeaked.

Wayne didn't have to answer Lily's question, or rather he couldn't. The ensuing splash told them that he'd ended up in water. After a few splats and bubbling noises came a long exhalation. "Bloody hell. Yeah, you're close. Just to warn you, there's a massive pool of water down here. It's pretty deep."

The tunnel opened up below into a large archway.

Harriet gulped hard. Now would be the time to admit she couldn't swim very well. There wasn't any getting out of it this time. No pulling sickies. She inched down the last three rungs of the ladder and stopped.

"Harri, jump in, man. What are you waiting for?" Tyrone groaned from above.

"Mate! By the time you get in I'll have grey hair and a beard," Wayne joked.

Lily butted in. "Harri, what is the matter?" If she could just turn around to see how deep the water was, she'd realise. All her energy was currently focused on hugging the rocks as tightly as she could.

The boys would laugh at her if she told them. It was alright for them; they could swim. She glanced down at the dirty, green water ebbing below her. Angry tears welled up in her eyes. Shallow water she could deal with, not deep water. She had two choices: either attempt to swim or confess to her friends that she couldn't do it. All eyes were fixed on her. One of them started whistling. Another laughed. Too much pressure. *Just go, Harri*, she snapped. She let go of the ladder and hit the stream with a hard splash; the cold water dragged her beneath its murky depths. She threw her arms above her head, slapping her hands against the water as her body ducked in and out of the surface. She'd forgotten the basic swimming stroke. Muffled screams bounced through her ears from above the surface. Water flooded through her nose, her mouth and her ears. A rush of water surged down her throat. She sank quickly, her lungs burning with a frantic need for air. A decayed woman's face hurtled up against Harriet's. Her mouth stretched open to the size of a tunnel, releasing a tormented wail. *Mohana is slipping away. My life is slipping away.* Numbness spread through her body; her heartbeat slowed down. The green laps of water and soundlessness was so soothing that she closed her eyes. Her feet touched the bottom. She couldn't breathe…

A sturdy arm wrapped across Harriet's chest, hauling her away from the bottom and back up to the surface. Choking up masses of water, Harriet let her head roll back onto the person's shoulder, her legs floating on the water's surface. She could just about see Wayne panting as he used his free arm to do a sidestroke; his face moved in and out of the water.

Once he'd swum several metres away from where they were, he stopped and guided Harriet onto a rotten wooden platform floating on the water. Her whole body trembled and he was quick to remove his hoodie and wrap it around her shoulders. He waited for her to get comfortable and catch her breath, all the time studying her with a mix of concern and frustration. His warm body breathed fast against her legs and he paused to exhale slowly.

"Are you OK?" he asked her. When she nodded in-between spluttering and gasping, he shook his head at her, swearing under his breath. "Might've been easier if you'd just told me you couldn't swim. You know that, right? I wouldn't have thought any less of you. Everyone sucks at something."

"I... sorry... I didn't want you to think I was stupid." Harriet pressed her trembling lips together. Warm tears spilled down her cheeks.

Wayne's brows drew together in a deep frown, but his eyes sparkled with humour. "I don't think you're stupid. Bit of a twat, maybe."

Harriet flicked a handful of water at Wayne, grinning as he scrunched up his face. She wasn't sure what made her do it – whether it was Wayne's kindness, the fact that she almost drowned or this whole situation – but she leant forwards and buried her head in Wayne's shoulder, letting her tears soak into his already soaked T-shirt. He didn't say anything. He hesitated, and eventually wrapped his arms around her, gently rubbing the small of her back.

Just as he did, that shooting pain zipped from her head into her stomach and she cried out, cuddling her middle. It felt a lot worse than all the other times, like someone ripping out her intestines. Wayne backed off, massaging his own stomach. Had he just experienced the same thing? It seemed to happen whenever they got close. She'd never experienced nerves like this before. Surely Wayne wasn't nervous? He didn't look the type.

"We should probably look for these bones," said Wayne, pressing his lips together. No smile, no nothing. Redness radiated from his bloodshot eyes. Whatever had just happened between them had now been forgotten, it seemed. He'd drifted further away from her in the water, barely looking at her. Did she say something wrong?

Lily and Tyrone soon caught up, treading the water as though it were second nature. The water was level with Lily's chin, but it didn't faze her. She'd removed her glasses, which explained why she wasn't focused on anything.

"I am so sorry, Harri. I didn't know the water was very deep. I can't believe there is not a rubber ring here," said Lily, smearing the water from beneath her nose.

"I can," said Tyrone, blinking around at the grimy walls. "It's not exactly a proper river, is it? It's just where all the dirty water's collected. It doesn't look like anyone's been down here for decades."

Lily fiddled with her rosary beads. "Where will be Mohana's bones? I don't see the time, but it must be nearly seven now."

"See that door, just behind Harri? I reckon it might be through there. I can't think where else it'd be," said Wayne, nodding towards a rotten lopsided, wooden door set above four crumbling steps leading out of the water. A thin shaft of light fell through the small gap between the uneven frame of the door and the decayed wall.

"Harri, you go first. You're closest," said Tyrone, nodding towards the door.

Or was it because he was too scared to go first? Now wasn't the time to ask silly questions. *I started this, so I should finish it*, Harriet told herself. She rolled onto her front and crawled across the wooden platform towards the door, hesitating as it rocked beneath her weight. If Wayne, Lily and Tyrone hadn't gathered together to hold it steady for her, she might have fallen in again. As the steps drew closer, she practically leaped off the platform onto the second step, splaying her body against the rotten door to stop herself falling into the water. Instead, the wooden door swung open and she tumbled straight into a stony, sinister dungeon.

Dust floated everywhere, prickling Harriet's nose. She sneezed twice, rubbing a layer of grit from her eyes. The humidity made it difficult to breathe. Below the crumbling stone walls half buried in the gravel were piles of rubble, empty glass bottles, chipped jewels and tiny pebbles that kept digging into her shoes. Several scraggy rats scuttled along the edges of the dungeon and up the walls, looking like creatures that had just crawled out of a grave. One candle flame flickered within a glass jar hanging against the wall by the door. It didn't help that she had to bend her head to avoid scraping it on the low ceiling. Surely that flame hadn't been burning there since 1665? Then again, it was near the corpse of a witch. Nothing was impossible where magic was concerned.

"Were people, like, gnome-sized in the seventeenth century?" Tyrone moaned, bumping his head on the ceiling as he crept through the door.

Harriet barely heard him. A tall, human-shaped frame made up of iron bands hung from the highest ceiling in the dungeon. The words from the history book jogged Harriet's mind: *Use the key to open the iron cage… where bugs feast on human meat.* She was one hundred per cent sure that it was called a gibbet cage. It's where they used to publicly display corpses of criminals and the crows would go and peck at their flesh. Most of the gruesome stuff she'd learnt from Dad.

"*Oh, dios mío!* Have you found the bones?" Lily whispered, standing by the doorway. She couldn't bring herself to walk any further into the dungeon.

Harriet didn't speak, or rather she couldn't find her voice. A strange guttural noise came out instead and she patted the phlegm from her hammering chest. Her friends froze in silence as she reached for the oil lamp hanging on the wall and tiptoed back across to the cage. Battling to keep her quivering hand steady, she raised the lamp up against the corroded bars of the cage and pressed her face between the gaps.

# FOURTEEN

# HISTORY UNLOCKED

The candlelight cast its glow onto the gibbet cage. Heaped on the cage floor were the discoloured bones of a human skeleton. Beside it lay a thick piece of rope. It was tied into a large loop, where thirteen coils secured it in place. Dried blood stained the coils. Wrapped around the loop were strands of black hair.

"Mohana!" Harriet set the oil lamp on the ground and went to yank at the gibbet door when her eyes fell onto the large keyhole with an odd slot that looked like a crocodile's jaw. Almost automatically, she delved into her sopping wet satchel and fumbled around, until her fingers curled around a sharp, cold, jagged object. Her hands shook as she held the old key up to the keyhole. It didn't fit into the hole as easily as she'd hoped. She had to twist it, jerk it and ram it before it finally slotted in, and even then it was a chore to turn the key sideways. It probably hadn't been used for hundreds of years. It was a miracle it fitted in at all.

*Clunk.* The key jolted to the left so fiercely that it nearly threw Harriet to the ground. It took three tugs to pull the key back out and another three tugs to actually wrench open the door.

Behind her, she could hear her friends talking in hushed tones. Probably about her. There wasn't any time to check on them right now. The time on her phone watch told her it'd just gone half seven. Had they really been down here that long? An hour and a half.

She leant into the cage and stared at the pile of bones on the cage floor. What did she expect? Of course the bones wouldn't still be intact after four hundred years. A cold tremor raced through her body. She'd never touched a real skeleton before. It crossed her mind to ask Wayne or Tyrone to collect the bones, but then she didn't want to be seen as gutless. *You can do this, Harri.* She reached in and carefully lifted the cold, lumpy skull out of the cage, screwing her eyes as though it might help block it out.

"Dude, there's an old sack here. Put the bones in this," said Tyrone, setting down a brown hessian sack beside Harriet. He took one look at the skull and retreated to the others.

How kind of him to help. She didn't need him anyway. In fact, the more bones she scooped out, the easier and quicker it became. She'd expected the sack of bones to be a lot heavier – not less than ten pounds. Mohana must've been an extremely small woman. It made things easier anyway. She removed the final bone from the gibbet cage and placed it in the sack…

A loud rumble beneath interrupted the awkward silence. Everything around them vibrated with aggression. Outside the dungeon, large pieces of rubble toppled down the tunnel and crashed into the pool below.

"What's happening?" Tyrone flinched.

"We've… I moved the bones. I've fully woken the curse. We need to get out of here!" Harriet swallowed hard, throwing quick glances around her. The archaeologists had the right idea by not even entering the tunnel.

Lily stormed over to Harriet. Her face twisted into what could only be described as extreme rage. "THIS is your fault. If we didn't have magic, then we would right now be in the main village, getting ready for Halloween like all the normal people. But because of you – we are stuck here. In this mess."

…OK… Where did that come from? Did they all think the same thing? "Look, you agreed to come here. It's not like I forced you. You can make your own choices. For once, why don't you just use your brain?" Already Harriet regretted her words. She could see the hurt in Lily's eyes.

Lily stiffened her posture, pursing her lips. "YOU are the one without a brain. I thought we are friends, but you have just proved me wrong."

"…Harsh." Wayne looked from Lily to Harriet.

Harriet gritted her teeth. She couldn't look Lily in the eye. Then it all came out. "You want to talk about friendship? I know that you went to Jazz's house party without telling me. She couldn't wait to show me photos. What sort of friend does that make you?"

Both boys shuffled uncomfortably, keeping their heads down. They certainly couldn't talk. They'd also been at the party.

"Look, I never tell you about it because Jazz didn't want you there. You don't like Jazz anyway, so why are you caring?" Lily was screaming now, her English worsening. "Instead of yelling at everyone else, look in the mirror and ask why you have no friends, why we are in this mess, why all the time you act like a spoilt child. Oh wait – you are."

Harriet couldn't think of anything to say. Is this what the boys thought too? She knew she shouldn't have involved the others. Biggest mistake of her life. She didn't want to share her theory about Jazz being possessed by Silas, especially not now. Her friends wouldn't believe her. They'd think she was being immature because she disliked the bleached-blonde Barbie doll.

None of them knew why these two spirits had truly come back to take revenge on one another. None of them knew how Silas died. Maybe Mohana had had something to do with it. It could be that neither of them was in the wrong – or in the right. Whatever the answer, the two spirits wouldn't rest until they'd taken revenge on each other – but why?

The candle in the oil lamp fluttered so fervidly that it collapsed into a swirl of smoke.

Darkness shrouded the dungeon. Harriet spun around to where she figured the wooden door might be. She couldn't be sure if her friends were still standing there, but in that same area were a pair of red lights. Bright and round like human eyes. They were getting bigger. Nearer.

One single voice rasped in her ear. It was deep, aggressive. "Deliver the bones to the Fair by nine o'clock to end this curse."

Behind her, rats squealed; something like a rope swung back and forth.

Harriet clutched the sack of bones tighter. Could Jazz be hiding in here somewhere? There was that instruction again – deliver the bones to the Fair. That voice didn't belong to Mohana. It hadn't come from Harriet's head. It'd come from someone else. What if Lily was right and it belonged to Silas? Mohana's words triggered her memory: *Your choice will influence how it ends.* Did that mean if she chose to bury the bones, she'd live, and if she delivered the bones to the Fair, then she'd die?

Around her, rubble within the dungeon began to

plummet and smash to the trembling ground. Her friend's shrieks blasted through her ears. It's like the world had momentarily paused and someone just pressed play again. She checked her watch. Eight o'clock. One hour. A wave of panic swept through her tense body.

"It's going to take us too long to go out the way we came in," said Harriet, gesturing to the water and the tunnel. "We don't have time."

"So what are you suggesting then? We are going to die!" Lily screamed in her face. It was then that her emotions won the better of her. Eyes blazing bright gold, she hurled her arms up and down, shrieking like a madwoman. An intense orange glow lit up her fingertips. A fierce gale erupted from her fingers and whooshed above their heads, raging around the dungeon like a tornado. Cracks appeared between the bricks in the walls, causing them to separate and hurtle across the dungeon. Bricks and rubble were now flying all over the place. One brick plummeted straight for Lily's head. Wayne dived to catch it in his arms. His eyes then shot to Harriet and he dashed towards her, shouting what sounded like, "Bend down!"

Something hard and sharp struck Harriet's forehead. Everything around her swayed, the ground sloped downwards. A streak of wet dribbled down her head and she tottered backwards. *She's using her magic against me. Did she just throw that at me?* Harriet gasped, staring down at the brick that'd just

hit her head. Or was it a bri
when it kept moving in and ou

"Calm down, you absolute fre
and he stepped behind Lily, wrapp
around her body so that she could
hands dropped by her sides and the
She sobbed something in Spanish,                    hair
sweep over her face. She didn't apologise. Obviously
she wasn't sorry.

From above, a window of moonlight filtered into
the dungeon where all the bricks and slabs had fallen
out. Fresh night air spilled into the room. A wave of
chatter passed over the gap and then it went silent. In
all her anger, Lily had unintentionally done them all
a favour. At least this new escape route didn't involve
wading through deep water.

Was that Tyrone climbing up the walls or was it
Wayne? No, it was Tyrone. Harriet narrowed her eyes,
massaging the tightness that lingered in her head. She
blinked several times, trying to get rid of the blurry
film coating her eyes.

"This is basically rock climbing, but without the
ropes," mumbled Tyrone, grabbing a rock to heave
his body upwards. He'd just reached halfway. Lily
wasn't far behind him. She was so small and agile that
she made it look super easy.

Wayne scuffed his trainer against the floor and
looked at Harriet, gesturing his arm to the rocky wall.
"After you then."

m I sposed to climb up there with s skeleton? I can't… I want… it's…" Harriet's d suddenly felt too heavy for her neck. Tiredness had sucked away all her energy. The rocky walls, the bag of bones in her arms, Wayne's face, all turned black. The ground hurtled towards her face at a terrifying speed. "…Wa… Wayne, please take the bones. Take them to the… the graveyard. Meet me a… at the fake gravesto…"

Her eyelids drooped shut.

# FiFTEEN

# PLAGUED BY THE PAST

Strong winds nibbled at Harriet's face. The ground didn't feel cold and flat anymore, but hard, bumpy and sludgy. Water splashed as she stretched her legs out in front of her. Her socks were now clinging to her feet. The smell of fresh hay plunged right down Harriet's throat. Somewhere in front of her, horses' hooves and wheels grated across the ground. Mud splattered onto her face and she cringed.

This wasn't the dungeon. She flipped open her eyelids.

She recognised that smoky smell anywhere. Hard cobbles dug into her back and she struggled into a sitting position. Olde Pie Streete looked different at night. The stalls just black shapes dotted along the street. Broomsticks, rotten food and an abandoned cartwheel were propped against the corner of the Washerwoman's Hut.

Harriet rubbed the faint dull ache still pounding in her head. A long length of rope, stained with dried blood and black hair, was secured around her waist. Oh God. That was Mohana's noose. Her fingers shook as she desperately struggled to untie the knot. It was too tight. Wayne must've used it to hoist her out of the dungeon, but it didn't make sense why he'd left her in the middle of the street. She wrung the dirt from her hands and stood up, talking to no one in particular. "Where is everyone? Wayne? Tyrone?"

As if in answer, a cart rumbled to a halt outside the Blacksmith's Hut opposite her. Painted on the door was a large red cross. Below were the words *Lord have mercy upon us*. That didn't used to be there. Or did it?

Two bulky men tramped towards the hut, bellowing, "Bring out your dead! Bring out your dead!" They left the hut carrying a lifeless body outside, dragging it onto the cart. It was Dave, the actor who played the blacksmith. Beneath him were about twenty other bodies, covered in ravenous rats. The Plague? That wasn't on the Halloween line-up.

Harriet spent a couple of minutes trying to find her voice. "…I… I don't think anyone's acting anymore. Something doesn't feel right."

She walked along the cobbled street littered in what looked like real animal carcasses. It stank worse than a sewer. She sped up her pace, bowing her head against the winds. Across the street, three black rats scampered down the gutter of an alleyway. Where were all these rats coming from?

Footsteps tramped behind her.

Harriet spun around. Rain splattered against the cobblestones. Rubbish skated across the street. Shadows skulked in alleyways. "Hello? Lily?"

The footsteps returned. There were more of them this time.

"Hello?" Harriet called again, throwing glances around her.

Nothing.

Harriet broke into a brisk walk, heading straight for the narrow archway. Behind her, the footsteps sounded close. The tall trees surrounding the castle swished. Their branches snatched the wind like witches' fingers.

The footsteps stopped.

Harriet bit her sore lip. Something told her not to turn around, but she couldn't help it. She turned her head.

Glazed eyes. That's all she could see in the darkness. Then the faces became clear: Ben, Molly the costume lady, Laura the milkmaid and several others she recognised as staff.

Harriet's breath caught in the back of her throat. She closed her eyes. *Please go away. This isn't happening. This isn't happening.* When she opened her eyes, she was met by darkness, shapes and the silhouettes of huts. The faces had disappeared.

The blurriness began to clear from Harriet's head. All the panic she'd felt earlier ricocheted back. Her eyes bulged. She hastily prodded her watch. Eight ten. Only fifty minutes to bury the bones. Her arms were empty. The bones! Her breathing sped up. Then she remembered. Wayne had the bones. She'd asked him to take them to the graveyard. Maybe that's why he'd left her in the street, so that he could try and complete the task, as she'd asked. Their time restraints meant that he couldn't hang around and wait for her to wake up from whatever weird state she'd been in.

She spun around and raced down Magpie Lane, away from the crowd. Numbness spread up her arms. *The entire village are under the influence of Silas's power. He is controlling everyone, just like he did back then*, the inner voice rasped. *His identity will soon manifest itself. Do not trust anyone. Beware.*

Did that mean she'd soon come face to face with Jazz?

Harriet had never felt so alone. It hurt to think that Tyrone and Lily had quit the task. At least Wayne had stuck by her. He'd probably be at the graveyard by now, waiting for her by the fake grave. Harriet knew she should be relieved. They'd complete the task by nine o'clock and then everything would go back to normal.

Something inside just wouldn't stop niggling at her. Mohana's words rang through her head: *Bury the bones, together... Unite, or die.* Together, meaning all four friends together. Not just two of them. Their powers were strongest when they united, when they worked together. Beads of sweat trickled down Harriet's head. She had to find them.

The bedroom window of the Shoemakers burst open.

An old woman leant over the ledge. She tipped out the contents of a chamberpot before slamming the windows shut. That was not just water. Harriet hopped backwards, away from the watery brown lumps trickling towards her shoes.

Gross. That smelt like real... She wrinkled her nose.

She turned around, nearly bumping into an actor dressed as a night watchman. He staggered past, yelling, "Quarter past eight and all's well!" He raised his staff and oil lamp in the air, eyes gleaming.

*But it's not all well*, she wanted to say.

There was a cough from the window above and somebody whispered.

Footsteps tramped towards her in the darkness.

She tensed.

"Hello, Harri," whispered a boy's voice.

Lily and Tyrone stepped forwards. Thank goodness for that. Despite them both quitting on her, it felt good to see some familiar faces. Harriet let her shoulders slacken. She couldn't decide whether to be angry or relieved to see them.

Tyrone had changed back into his barber surgeon outfit. His eyes stared through her.

Lily brushed the dust from her dress. She wasn't the same chirpy Lily that Harriet knew. Something had changed. In both of them.

Harriet decided she'd better talk first seeing as no one else was bothering. "Erm. I'm off to the graveyard. Are you guys coming?"

"No," said Lily, her voice flat, monotone.

"OK… I'll try again. You have to come. The four of us need to bury these bones. Together. I'm sorry about what I said in the dungeon," Harriet pressed.

Tyrone paced towards her. "We don't need to do anything *together*."

"Guys, come on. We are going to die if we don't complete this task. Wayne needs our help," Harriet insisted. She didn't have the time or the patience for this.

"Wayne wasn't needing our help. He tell us to go and wait inside. I think he will be back soon." Lily glared at Harriet.

"Inside where?" Harriet flung her arms out.

"The Shakespeare Inn, of course. We'll be safe in there," Tyrone added.

"From Silas, you mean?" Harriet took a step back.

Lily let out a sound that could've been a giggle. "No. From you. In twenty minutes you will be dead."

Harriet slunk backwards. Although she didn't want to admit it to herself, both Tyrone and Lily had fallen under Silas's control. She had to help Wayne bury the bones before it was too late. He was probably just being kind by telling Tyrone and Lily to stay in the warm while he did all the hard work.

"Where is Jazz… has she been possessed by Silas? Or is one of you Silas?" Harriet stammered. She had to ask. Those red eyes and the aggressive voice in the dungeon were surely a sign that Silas had been in there. Although if they were possessed by Silas, surely she would have sensed it – or rather Mohana would have sensed it. She hadn't a clue how Mohana would react when Silas did finally present himself.

Tyrone laughed this time. He didn't show any sign of recognition or pity. "Come with us. We've got something to show you. I think you'll like it."

No way. Harriet spun on her heel and ran in the direction of the church, crunching on a heap of shattered lamps lying on the ground behind her. The winds were now vicious.

The courtyard narrowed into a wide street, overlooked by jagged timber-framed buildings. Every other door dripped with a red cross. Further in the distance, dozens of footsteps pounded against the cobbles, growing louder and closer on each step. The whole village was after her. She sped up her pace, nearly tripping over a young boy crawling around on his hands and knees, sneezing and coughing blood, reaching out an arm to Harriet. She didn't have time to stop. She didn't want to stop. She didn't know what was going on, what the Plague had to do with anything. She hurried on. The street curved to the right, where more victims lay spluttering on the ground. Some of them clawed their way towards the inn on the left.

The time on her phone hit eight thirty. Half an hour left before her time was up. She just hoped Wayne had managed to find the fake grave. They'd then have to figure out where to bury the bones. Her arms numbed; the inner voice spoke again: *Trust and forgiveness is the key. We must all be at one for us to rest. Mine is his. His is mine. Our bones must be together.*

What? Their bones must be together? Whose bones?

She didn't have time to figure it out. She had to get to the graveyard, and quick. Luckily it was a straight run from the Ale House, through Shire Square Market and along Magpie Lane. A pair of heels and pattering feet clacked somewhere behind her, but she didn't have time to stop. Eyes glared through windows, shadows skulked in alleyways, the rain poured hard and fast. Another couple of rats scampered past her feet. A wonky sign pointing to Hallows Hill Church sped past on her left. Nearly there.

It suddenly made sense. These rats were spreading the Plague. The Plague happened in 1665 – the year that Silas reigned. The year that Mohana died. The village had become seventeenth-century Hallows Hill. A place of torture, evil and death. Everyone had been sucked back to 31st October 1665. This wasn't Mohana's doing – it was Silas: part of his curse, part of his revenge. If Harriet failed to bury the bones, she would become part of the curse. All this mixed in with Harriet and her friends reading the verse that had resurrected their spirits and disturbing Mohana's bones at the dungeon. Today, just over four hundred years ago, Mohana fell to her death after losing her battle against evil. Harriet felt it her duty to change the outcome… somehow. She now regretted her lack of interest in history. Those common proverbs like history repeating itself and the past coming back to haunt people meant a lot more to her than they ever had done. Maybe it proved that people had to be at peace with their past before moving on?

Harriet's feet trampled on the familiar wild grass. Her shoes sunk into the damp mud. Branches clawed at her coat as she treaded quickly through the silent graveyard, being careful not to trip again. She headed towards the front of the church, where she'd found Mohana's gravestone two nights ago. Her breaths became pants. She could see it, just beyond that bramble bush. A ray of moonlight splashed onto the faded epitaph on the crumbling stone – just like it had when she first saw it.

Her pulse sped up. She hurdled over a mass of weeds, skirted around the bramble bush and skidded to a halt at the crumbly grave.

No Wayne. No bones. No footprints.

## SiXTEEN

# THE MASKED
# DANCERS

Harriet called Wayne's number six times. She was greeted by the message, "The number you have called is not recognised. It has not been possible to connect your call. Please try again later." *What's going on? It's the right number*, she stressed. Even worse, the screen of her phone watch now read, 'Mobile network not available'. What if the group who'd been chasing her had found Wayne and the bones first? Harriet struggled to breathe properly. What now? Right at that moment she wanted Mum. She even considered calling Dad, but there was no way he'd believe her. She was alone. No friends. No family.

According to Tyrone, most of the village would be in the Shakespeare Inn. Perhaps that's where Mum,

Jazz, Wayne and Mohana's bones would be. She wasn't entirely sure this was a good idea. Something in the pit of her stomach told her to stay away from the inn. What choice did she have? Where else was she supposed to go?

The Shakespeare Inn on Fish Street was at the other end of the village. That's originally where the Halloween Masked Ball was going to take place. Surely it wouldn't happen now, with all this going on. Taking one last look around the graveyard for Wayne and the sack, she headed back through the brambles and bushes, using the torch on her watch to lead the way. She took the route that led her out onto Old Pie Streete. Every building was veiled in sinister shadows. Her brisk walk sped into a run. She'd never run this fast in her life. The path curved to the left onto Goulding Lane. The Coffee House didn't look as inviting as it had done this morning. It only seemed like five minutes ago she was inside discussing Mohana and Silas with her friends. So much had happened within a day.

Harriet pulled her Eskimo hood over her head and hurried through a maze of dark, dank alleyways, where crooked houses jutted over her. Hanging shop signs creaked and groaned, and a wet rat scuttled past the feet of a shadow that stood beneath the smoky beam of an oil lamp.

Harriet stopped. "W-who's there?"

The rat squealed. Harriet stepped closer to the oil lamp and strained her eyes, trying to identify the stranger leant against the wall by a drainpipe. The figure, who hadn't yet noticed her, mumbled something under their breath. Thunder growled. The mumbling stopped. Two red lights shone brightly – like the ones in the dungeon.

"…Jazz?" she barely whispered.

The voice in Harriet's head warned her to act quickly. Her stomach twisted. Even though a tiny part of her wanted to know who this stranger could be, the better part wanted to get as far away as possible. She let out a noise somewhere in-between a scream and a whimper. *Everyone's out to get me*, she panicked. Her hair flew all over the place as she struggled through the windstorm up an alleyway, grabbing a nearby lantern hanging outside the Chocolate House on Peasant's Walk. Not once did she look back.

She didn't have long.

Peasant's Walk steered her onto Fish Street. Only yesterday it'd swarmed with guests. Now it was derelict, apart from the shuffling of feet near the fishmongers. It took a few seconds for Harriet's eyes to adjust to the dark. At that moment, she focused on the outline of a person standing motionless in the shadows ahead, staring at her with eyes that were gleaming red lights. She couldn't stop the small cry from leaving her lips. Was this the same person she'd seen about five minutes ago on Goulding Lane? Her arms turned numb. The voice in her head grew more powerful: *YOUR TIME IS ALMOST UP.*

Harriet could practically hear her heart thumping. Every muscle in her body tensed. She tore her eyes from the glaring stranger and made a dash towards the Shakespeare Inn. She thought they might follow her. They didn't.

She buried her face beneath her furry hood and stooped beneath the low oak-beamed ceiling. She didn't want to show any fear. If she blended in, then hopefully any possessed staff or guests wouldn't clock her.

The low din of dramatic classical music hummed in the background. Every face hid behind masks of ghosts, monsters, zombies. Halloween was actually still happening.

One of these people could be Silas.

Tonight, that person planned to kill Harriet and her friends if they failed to bury the bones on time.

From the corner of her eye, Harriet became aware that somebody was trooping towards her. As the masked dancers parted, a tall, redheaded woman dressed in a navy-blue suit and skirt clip-clopped out her fury on the floorboards. Mum. Bet she was going to yell at Harriet for disappearing all afternoon. For once, she didn't care. She'd never been so glad to see Mum.

But Mum said nothing. She just stood there.

"Mum, sorry I've been gone for ages. I had something important to do," said Harriet.

Mum cocked her head to one side. "Like stealing the bones of a criminal?"

How did she know?

"Mohana isn't a criminal, Mum. She was a witch. She helped heal people," Harriet jumped in, clutching her mum's hand. "Look, I'm really sorry that I didn't tell you about any of this. I didn't think you'd believe me. Mum, you have to help us."

Mum tore her hand from Harriet's clutches and blinked. Her eyes changed. They completely glazed over. "Why should I help you? Tonight you will meet your end, and you have helped that happen. Witch."

Harriet lost her voice. Everything inside her felt tight, crumpled. Her legs refused to move. "…Mum?"

"You are no child of mine." Her deep voice boomed through the inn.

"M-M-Mum…" Harriet couldn't move anymore. She let her body collapse to the ground. All the energy had been sucked out of her. She tucked her head in-between her knees, rocking back and forth. What was the point anymore? Now she didn't have anyone. She shut her eyes and cried harder than she ever had before. "I want my mum back. I'm sorry for everything. I don't care about you and Ben. Please, just come back."

Harriet fought to swallow. How could this be happening? It was just one long nightmare. She'd wake up any moment in her soft bed with the stripy blue duvet and Zeke, the teddy, by her feet. The TV in the corner of the room, clothes from yesterday sprawled across the floor. Posters of her favourite bands plastered over the walls. Mum calling her down for breakfast. Yep, home. Yet a minute passed and the situation hadn't changed. Her home was miles away.

She glanced up. How long had that red-masked guy been standing over her? He grabbed her by the hand and led her to a corner of the pub. One arm slithered across her waist while his white-gloved hand locked around her fingers. He whirled her beneath his arm and she tilted her head back.

"You look worried. Are you wondering where the bones are? Everything will be fine. The bones are being prepared for destruction – and soon, you will join them," the rasping voice beneath the mask murmured in her ear.

"Tyrone? Is that you? Are you Silas?" Harriet gasped. The deep laugh mingled with the background clatter and the whole inn spun round and round, melding everything into a fuzzy blur. The stranger let her go.

Blood gushed around Harriet's head. She scrunched her eyes, doddering sideways, desperate to sit down. A pair of hands clutched Harriet's wrists. She opened her eyes.

A new partner stepped forward and arched into a bow, their face disguised by a crinkly zombie mask.

"So I have you to thank for trying to get rid of me. Nice try, darlin'." The bitter voice of a twisted face behind the mask spoke. The woman traced her red fingertips across Harriet's throat and lurched forwards, howling with laughter when Harriet jumped back. The washerwoman, Lottie Jessop. Wayne must've brought her back from Zimbabwe. Was she Silas? Confused wasn't the word right now.

The zombie-masked washerwoman edged backwards.

The music turned up to the loudest notch. Out went the lights.

"Wait…" Harriet trailed off.

She now stood in complete darkness, not knowing where to go or what to do. *Is this it?*

A heavy hand slammed against her back. Two red lights glowed back at her. She could taste the perfume on their ragged costume. Feel their breath as they leant into her ear. A cold mask touched her skin. The pain inside her became unbearable.

"Look after your stuff more carefully. Trust no one." The stranger swung her around, tossed her backwards and flipped her up against their chest like a ragdoll. A voice breathed into her ear. "I am Silas, unfortunate son of Mohana. It won't be long before I take revenge on her for my death. That means – *you die.*"

Harriet's wide-eyed expression was overshadowed by the inner voice that tainted her tone and expression. Her whole body froze. Her mouth moved, but she couldn't control what came out of it. "You had what was coming, Silas."

Harriet flexed the feeling back into her arms and legs. Her body belonged to her again. Wait. What?

Silas was Mohana's son? No way. All this time. So Mohana killed him. But how? He died after she did. She closed her eyes and remembered Mohana's words: *Trust and forgiveness is the key. We must all be at one for us to rest. Mine is his. His is mine. Our bones must be together.* Those words. She'd seen them before. With a trembling hand, she lifted her phone watch and swiped to the photo of Mohana's fake gravestone with the foreign spell. She raised her wrist up to the gleam of moonlight glowing through the window and watched as the letters switched places to form the English text. That was the true meaning of the spell. Now it made sense. Silas and Mohana's bones had to be buried together. Mother and son. They had to forgive each other before being at peace. That was the key.

Light swamped back into the room.

Harriet threw glances around her. The strangers were closing in on her.

Laughter rippled through the inn, starting softly and getting louder. But behind all the action, beside a pillar stood the most grotesque thing Harriet had ever seen. Blood poured from a woman's clothing, her mouth and her hair. Chunks of flesh hung loose from her face. Her nails had been ripped out. She whistled the harpsichord tune.

"*Bury our bones before it's too late. Let this be your final warning. My death is coming back to haunt you.*"

"I know you've been possessed by Silas, Jazz! Give me the bones!" Harriet shrieked.

Whispers circled the room. *Death is coming. Your time is up. Death is coming. Your time is up.*

Bones snapped. Mohana's head flopped to one side. Rainwater dribbled from the hem of her soaked dress.

Harriet couldn't see Mohana anymore. A mass of people swarmed around her like a pack of ravenous wolves. She couldn't speak. Everything mingled into a muffled echo. Nothing mattered anymore. Nobody could help her. She didn't know who to trust. Hallows Hill had returned for good. She'd failed Mohana. Silas had won.

A bulky man grabbed Harriet's arms and tied them together with rope, much to the delight of the crowd. "Harriet Flynn, by order of Silas Oakes..."

Harriet closed her eyes to the images that appeared in her mind. *She sees the gallows.*

"...you will be taken to a place of execution..."

*A girl in a thick winter coat and trousers dangles from the noose.*

"...where you will hang..."

*Legs kick and then stop.*

"...by your neck..."

*Blackness thins to reveal the pale lifeless face of...*

"...until you are dead..."

*Harriet.*

"...at precisely nine o'clock tonight. May the lord have mercy on your soul."

# SEVENTEEN

# SIX-FOOT DROP

People lined the streets, the balconies, the rickety steps. Others drooped out of windows, jeering and shouting at the passing captive in the horse-driven wooden cart, throwing food and chanting, 'Witch! Witch! Witch!'

She imagined this would be what it felt like to play a villain in a pantomime. The minute they walk on stage, they're booed, hissed, hated. She'd become the hated villain here, not Silas. From where she sat, Harriet could see a tall wooden construction further ahead. The platform was around ten feet long by eight feet wide. It looked like a large box with two parallel beams. She'd seen pictures of the gallows during Miss Keane's history lessons, but never did she imagine she'd be staring at the real thing. Not once did she think that the girl hanging from a noose in her dream would be her.

Everybody had piled into Shire Square to watch the event like it was some sort of celebration. Throngs of people shuffled backwards to allow the captive to trundle to her final destination. Right at the front was Jazz, staring up at Harriet wearing a hideous smirk. If only Harriet hadn't wished to bring Jazz back from her shrivelled-up state. It would have made burying the bones a whole lot easier.

Harriet had to stop her. She had to stop Silas. She couldn't think about what might happen. It didn't feel like she was about to die. The thought that she may no longer exist in half an hour wouldn't register. It sounded so final. She wasn't ready. What if she tried wishing herself out of here? Would Wayne be able to grant it from wherever he was?

*I wish I was home in London*, she begged.

She waited. Nothing. Her heart sank.

Eight fifty.

Two older men hauled Harriet out of the wooden cart and led her up the shaky wooden steps leading onto the platform of the gallows. Her legs wouldn't work properly. She struggled to force them up the steps, against their will. Her brain refused to agree with what she wanted her body to do – move closer to its death. A steady drum roll procession began. Each strike of the wooden stick on the hollow drum grew louder than the jeering of the crowd. The masked executioner guided Harriet into position over the trapdoor, sliding a noose around her neck. Its rough fibres scraped against her skin.

Harriet couldn't think properly right now. So many things buzzed around her mind, though too quick for her to absorb. She felt helpless. If she looked down for too long her insides melted into liquid. She didn't need to see below to know that there were thousands of people waving fire torches in the air, shouting names at her. She'd lost the ability to form any words. How would she stop this from happening? She had to get rid of Jazz somehow, who had now started leaping in the air with excitement. Where were Lily and Tyrone? How could she stop them from being under Silas's control? Where was Wayne?

Alan Hardy, the village photographer now dressed as a priest, stepped forward with a long sheet of parchment, smirking at the prisoner. "Harriet Flynn, you will accept the consequences of your unlawful crimes that have endangered the population of this village."

"Wayne, where are you?" Harriet uttered.

Alan glared at her; his snarl dripped with pride. "Wayne is dead."

Her insides turned cold. No. He was lying to her. Wayne wasn't dead. He couldn't be dead. She only saw him a little while ago. Alan was just trying to frighten her. If Alan was lying, then where was Wayne? Why hadn't he been with Lily and Tyrone? She hadn't seen him since leaving the dungeon. Perhaps it was time to face the truth. One of the possessed people must've grabbed him just as he was burying the bones and… killed him. Her chest sank. Tears rolled down her cheeks. Mohana never warned her that her friend would die. Only Dad could save her now – if he was here. He wasn't affected or possessed like everyone else. He'd never get back from France in time and he'd never leave his comatose brother just like that anyway, not for something that sounded like a Halloween prank to him. She cast a quick glimpse below her. The spectators watched with a delicious anticipation. Others strutted through the bustle and noise selling food and drink, all in preparation for the public execution they were about to witness. She fought to swallow the saliva that had mounted up in her mouth.

"By order of Mayor Silas, duly appointed representative of His Majesty the King…" Alan Hardy continued.

Time was running out. A hollow ache rumbled in the pit of Harriet's stomach. She wheezed in each breath. Then it all began to feel strangely familiar as the numbness pricked at her feet, working its way up. Sweat smothered her boiling hands. She daren't glance down at the marked trapdoor beneath her feet. A trickle of sweat raced down the bridge of her nose. Strands of black hair whipped her face in the breeze, wrapping itself around the thick rope. Rain attacked her face, soaking her black dress and forming a puddle beneath her tatty boots.

*Mohana*, she screamed inside.

Across the courtyard, she could see a cloaked figure with red eyes, hiding in the shadows, carrying something in its arms. It waited for the moment that would change Hallows Hill forever. It couldn't even watch. The coward. Even though she 'repulsed' him, he couldn't bear to face the consequences of his actions.

Hang on… if Jazz was standing below her, then who was the figure with red eyes?

"…punishment for witchcraft and conspiracy. For these crimes, you shall hang by the neck until dead."

Harriet could hear nothing but her rapid, deep breaths.

Eight fifty-five. In five minutes, Harriet would drop six feet. Silas was trying to prevent her from burying the bones at nine o'clock so that he could burn them. *Come on, Harri, get with it*, she yelled at herself. What about using magic? It could release her in an instant. Maybe Mohana tried using her powers but failed. This time, it was going to work.

She gritted her teeth and chose to focus on the muddy patch of ground below where no one was standing. Her concentration whizzed all over the place. It wasn't easy with all the drums, the crowds and their noise. Her eyes hadn't started stinging yet. *Come on, release me. Release me*, she demanded. It was no good. She couldn't focus. There was too much going on around her and in her head. She decided to try a different approach and closed her eyes. *Tyrone, Lily, please help me. Remember what's important. Our life, our friendship, how far we've come together. Silas doesn't care about any of you. He's going to kill you because you have magic powers. Don't let him control you. You're in charge. Trust and forgiveness is key*, she pleaded.

The church clock ticked. The drum roll struck. *Bom. Bom. Barom bom-bom-bom. Bom. Bom. Barom bom-bom-bom. Bom... Bom... Ba... rom... bom... bom...* The drum roll slowed right down to a crawl. Silence blanketed the square. The crowd practically paused mid-action. Even the executioner behind her froze with his hands clutching the lever. She couldn't hear the ticking of the clock anymore.

"What...?" Harriet gasped.

"Psst, Harri," a voice hissed in her ear. Whoever it was seemed to be fiddling with the noose. "Dude, it's Tyrone. Lily's here too. We're gonna get you out, yeah? Need to be quick, though. I can't keep this magic going for much longer. I've actually frozen everyone."

Harriet wanted to cry, scream and laugh all at once. "Thank you! I'm so glad you're here." She poked her fingers through one of the coils in the noose in an attempt to help Lily and Tyrone release her.

"Why you are having a rope around your waist?" Lily stammered, tugging at the noose.

"Wayne – it doesn't matter." Harriet coughed as her friends jerked at the rope.

The church clock ticked once. The drum beat once. Tyrone's powers were weakening.

The crowd remained still, except for some movement at the other end of the courtyard. It was the figure that Harriet saw earlier, still carrying something in its arms. It didn't seem to be affected by Tyrone's powers. It just stood there, staring at her.

"I'm nearly done. This rope is proper tight," said Tyrone, jerking the noose about, his hands shaking, eyes pure gold.

All at once, a dark weight cloaked Harriet's numb body. Black hair flew in every direction. She glared across at the figure, clenching her teeth. The mayor. She pointed a finger at the shaded outline.

"*Yersinia pestis!*" She screamed the word to inflict the Plague. Lightning bolted from her finger and headed straight for the figure's body. They jerked backwards, losing control of their limp arms and legs. They collapsed to the ground. A mounting number of crows and rats piled on top of them, squealing in delight at the prospect of food.

The darkness and numbness lifted.

So Mohana did kill Silas, just before she fell to her death. She cursed him with the deadly pandemic that swept the village in 1665 – the Plague. Who had Harriet just cursed? Who had Silas possessed?

Mohana's words rang through her head.

*Betrayal is upon you.*

The red-eyed figure stood up and threw off its cloak. In its arms lay the sack of Mohana's bones.

No, it couldn't be! Harriet's chest throbbed. A stinging pain grated against the back of her swollen throat. Her eyes felt hot and puffy. She tried to speak, but it was all too much.

The jester raised his head and winked at Harriet, cradling the sack in his arms. His red eyes glared at her. "You're too late. You can't curse someone you have already cursed."

The ropes binding Harriet's wrists slackened. The noose around her neck slipped off her head. Harriet tumbled back onto the platform with a painful thud, choking and gasping for air. She couldn't feel her arms and legs. She tried to crane her head, but it felt like she'd snap every vein in her neck.

"We have to get those bones. We only have five minutes," Lily shrieked.

Noise. Lots of noise. Hundreds of feet trampled across the ground below the platform, getting thunderous, nearer. The noise turned into forceful voices, now clear enough to hear every word: 'Witch! Kill the Witch!'

Tyrone threw up his arms in defeat; his eyes switched back to green. "I tried to hold them off for as long as I could."

The whole crowd were coming for them.

"Wayne is Silas? I thought Jazz was… no, this can't be happening," Harriet managed to stammer. It wouldn't sink in.

Lily and Tyrone nodded, their expressions defeated.

The inner voice in her head growled, *BURY THE BONES or he will destroy you all.*

# EiGHTEEN

# THE TRUTH IS REVEALED

Tears pricked the back of Harriet's eyes. Something in her chest ached, felt heavy. The world around her slowed down to a crawl without the use of Tyrone's magic. Wayne had helped them find Mohana's bones. Wayne was her friend, or she thought he was. He used her, just like she'd originally thought. All this time, she'd been talking to Silas. She couldn't talk, even if she tried. Harriet's eyes jammed shut. A mixture of memories gushed through her head all at once, like a series of mismatched video clips.

*"I heard another voice, like a bloke's voice. He said, 'Deliver her bones to the Fair by nine. Burn Mohana.'"*

*Wayne wiped another streak of red dribbling down his lips, swearing to himself when it trickled onto his waistcoat. A glint of torment passed over his eyes, almost like he wanted to tell her something.*

*"You should probably stay away from me. I'm not a good person."*

Harriet choked. Wayne only helped her retrieve the bones so that she could deliver them to him at the appointed time for destruction. It wasn't Mohana who'd left the clues – it was Wayne. The only reason he got close to her was to prevent her from suspecting he'd been possessed by Silas. Only every time they'd got close, they were torn apart by the resentment felt by the spirits inside them. A thought then crossed Harriet's mind. If Wayne really was the user that she assumed him to be, then he could've recovered the bones himself. It made sense that Silas's spirit needed time to get stronger. It needed time to gain full control of Wayne, his thoughts and his actions. He began as an inner voice – a bit like Mohana had with Harriet.

Feeling the urge to throw something, she picked herself up from the gallows platform. Tyrone and Lily were standing close behind her, shifting uneasily.

Below them, the furious rabbles were rapidly approaching, wielding axes and pitchforks in the air. A hint of burning wood stung Harriet's nose. Smoke curled above the rooftops further ahead. Harriet's heartbeat hammered in her ears.

"Where is that smoke coming from?" Lily followed Tyrone down the narrow gallows steps, her legs kept buckling.

Harriet dug into her coat pocket and clutched the crinkled map. Strange how it'd remained unspoiled after enduring the trial underwater. Then again, it had been touched by cursed hands. Cautiously, she held it out in front of her, fighting to keep it still as it fluttered in the violent gust of wind and rain. "According to this map, the smoke's coming from the Fair."

"Doesn't Silas keep telling you to deliver the bones to the Fair?" Tyrone strained.

"Yes, and Wayne was the first person to hear that voice in his dream. Now we know why. The voice told him to burn Mohana's bones at the Fair," said Harriet, screwing up her eyes as the rain attacked her face.

"But why he is burning the bones at the Fair?" Lily trembled as she edged down the ladder.

Harriet pressed the map against her face, letting her eyes zoom in on the Fair. There was something written within the Fair, a place of interest. She blinked to get a better look. A sudden torrent of wind stole the map from her clutches and lured it into the air, swallowing it into the black night. Cursing the wind, she tried to visualise the Fair in her head. Apart from the attractions, what stood out most? *Silas obviously doesn't want Mohana's bones buried with him. He hates her and he hates her magic. He just wants rid of anything to do with her – which includes us. To him, we are all witches,* she muttered to herself. *Witches were hanged – and burned...*

"I've got it! The old stake; there's an old stake at the Fair. I walked past it on Friday night. He's going to burn his mum's bones!" said Harriet. She realised she was shouting now. This was partly because the crowd were now centimetres from the end of the ladder, battling to grasp Harriet and her friends as they neared the bottom.

"Wait, his mum?" Lily stopped.

Harriet had forgotten to tell them that part. She'd only really just found out herself.

"You two, we're gonna die before we even get to the bones," said Tyrone, pausing on the fourth step from the bottom and hurling out his shoe to knock a couple of aggressive men in the chin. "Whatever emotion I used to freeze time a minute ago, I can't do it again. I'm too freaked out right now."

Harriet had to try. Heat fired through her body and her eyes. Why did Silas feel the need to corrupt the minds of the whole village? Didn't he feel powerful enough to sort out his beef with Mohana by himself? Mohana clearly knew better. She only had four people on board – well, three now. They could do this. They didn't need Wayne. He'd got himself into this mess; he could get himself out. *Get out of our way*, Harriet gritted her teeth, glaring at the crowd below.

No sooner had she blinked, the crowd's bellows faded into the distance as their bodies flipped high into the air, bashing into the side of buildings or smacking into muddy puddles. That might've wounded them, but right now she didn't care.

"Right, quick. Let's run!" Harriet yelled, clambering down the ladder after Tyrone.

"Where? Which way did Wayne go?" Tyrone's eyes darted everywhere.

"Silas. It's Silas," Harriet corrected him. She couldn't bear to think about Wayne being possessed. She remembered all the things he'd done to her and it ripped her insides to pieces. "He was at the other end of the courtyard not long ago. He'll be heading to the Fair with Mohana's bones. We need to hurry. We can't let him burn her bones otherwise we become part of the curse. Three minutes!"

"Wait. Are we burying Mohana's bones in her fake grave?" Tyrone yelled.

"No, she has to be buried with her son, Silas!" Harriet called over her shoulder.

Tyrone panted heavily. "And where's that?"

A spark flared up in Harriet's mind. She'd nearly forgotten about the carved woman's hand on the fake grave and the carved man's hand on the cracked grave at the back of the churchyard. Lily's exact words were, "*Maybe it has been broken from the man's hand?*" The

157

two should be united in death. How did Harriet not see it before? Mohana and Silas's hands. The cracked grave contained Silas's bones. "The hands, Tyrone! The hands!"

"Huh? What are you on about?" Tyrone shouted.

"I think I understand what is she saying," Lily said, nodding towards Harriet.

Members of the crowd were gradually bounding back. That's when Lily lifted her glowing hands and expelled a handful of wind in their direction. It wasn't just wind; it was more like one of those tropical storms that are given standard names. The crowds slid backwards, battling to grab on to the nearest object. It reminded Harriet of the scene from *Mary Poppins*, only this situation was far from anything sweet and sugary.

Harriet raced ahead of her friends through Shire Square Market, hopping over the spilt apples and squashed pumpkins lying on the cobbles. The market led her into the courtyard and eventually through the deserted fair, which should've been heaving tonight. Instead, its only customers were a couple of scraggy rats, sniffing around the painted horses on the carousel. Harriet could hear her own footsteps slapping against the cobbles as she ran past the swingboat ride. Rain pelted at her head, splashing onto the hard cobblestones. If she wasn't careful, she'd slip and fall.

"Hey. Did you hear that?" Tyrone paused so abruptly that Lily bumped into him.

Harriet stopped at the sound of shoes pounding along the cobbles further up.

"Silas," she uttered. She couldn't explain how she knew. She recognised the footsteps, the deep, menacing laughter and the growling breaths. It was Silas. Without turning back to the others, she hurried past the big wheel and followed the heavy footsteps past the slide and towards a tight, dark alleyway where a pile of burning wood with a stake at the centre sat at the exit. The vibrant flames had already reduced half the pile to ashes. Smoke and embers danced through the air.

She deliberately blocked the exit to the alleyway. Something wriggled in her gut. Her heart thumped in her mouth.

Halfway down the alleyway, shoes scuffed against the cobbles. Her heart thumped harder, her breaths coming out in short, sharp pants. The outline of a figure wearing a jingly two-pointed hat paced towards her and stopped. Two red lights flashed back at her.

She stumbled backwards, out of the dark alleyway.

Lightning lit up the black clouds. Thunder clashed. The jester, in his motley jingly waistcoat and breeches, stood a few feet away from her, carrying the sack of bones. Black liquid seeped out from an apple-sized swelling on his cheek. There was one on his neck too. His fingernails had rotted to black. Purple and blue patches speckled his skin. He coughed. Blood sprayed from his mouth onto the ground. His entire eyeballs were red and he leered through a set of sharp, rotten teeth. There was nothing in Wayne's face that she recognised anymore.

From inside his waistcoat, the jester whipped out a balloon witch, like the one he'd made for Harriet yesterday. A snarl played on his lips as he grabbed the head and ripped it from the body. Black ashes poured from inside the balloon and he threw it to the ground, slamming his foot to pop the remaining air bubbles. He glowered at Harriet.

So he had made that balloon witch on purpose. If only she'd known then that a lot of Wayne's actions were warnings of his possession, like the bloodshot eyes. She'd even questioned it at the time but shrugged it off. It all started to make sense.

"Silas." Harriet became aware that her mouth had opened, but it wasn't her voice that came out. She wanted to hit him, scold him for all the grief he'd caused her and the entire village. Right now, she needed her bones. If he burnt the bones, he wouldn't be putting the curse to rest. Neither would he be destroying the magic or her spirit as he thought. He would be preventing the two of them from passing over to the other side. He would be destroying the four friends, burning their insides, leaving behind empty shells, their souls becoming part of the curse. This had to end at nine o'clock tonight. Their hour of death had to become their hour of harmony, freedom. War between them had to end. The curse had to be lifted.

Harriet understood. She could hear Mohana's thoughts as though they were her own. She didn't want to be a lost spirit, her life taken from her for trying to do the right thing. The object she needed was right before her very eyes, in the hands of the perpetrator. Her legs moved forwards effortlessly. She couldn't stop it. She didn't want to stop it.

Her lips moved again without her having to do anything, the voice croaky. "Silas, do you not question how you have managed to manipulate all the villagers into your way of thinking? How you managed to do it all those years ago?"

Silas's stare pierced her eyes. "I do not need to question myself. All the villagers believe that you worship the devil. You and your magic are evil."

"You manipulated them into believing that. And do you know how?" Mohana rasped.

"They already knew. They didn't need my help," Silas growled.

"MAGIC. That's how. You have the gift, as I do. You inherited it at birth," Mohana explained, her black hair flapping in the strong winds. "I never told you. I wanted you to find your own path, whether it be a life with or without magic. You chose to live without but used your powers without realising it."

"What rubbish. Get out of my way," Silas snarled.

Harriet allowed her body to mirror his. Her muscles were too numb to even scream at the beetle that slunk out of the deep gash in her cheek. She dreaded to think what she looked like right now. Surely not as horrifying as Wayne.

"Harri, we have four minutes. What you are doing?" Lily yelled. She could only see the back of Harriet.

Probably for the best.

"Silas, why do you think you have had so much power over Wayne? Where do you think his extra powers have come from?" Mohana asked.

Silas chuckled at this, forcing a nasty guttural sound with his throat. "That's easy. He was the most vulnerable host in the group. It turns out that the boy also hates his mother. A common theme, I see."

"Psst, Harri, do you need – should we do something?" Tyrone tiptoed closer to Harriet, placing a quivering hand on her shoulder. The moment she turned to look at him, he screamed using all the power in his lungs. Her hideous reflection glistened in his eyes. She wanted to tell him it was OK, but the words wouldn't come out. Mohana had taken control, just like Silas had with Wayne.

Tyrone's sudden noise provoked something in Silas. The jester's face warped into an ugly mess. He gestured for Tyrone to go away by flicking his hand, but by doing that, he sent Tyrone speeding over the burning stake and into a wooden pillar. Silas stared at his hand.

"Tyrone," Lily gasped. Clutching her rosary beads, she treaded forwards until she was standing against Harriet's back. She took one look at Wayne and hissed at him. "¡Lárgate, monstruo malvado!"

Silas peered over Harriet's shoulder and wriggled his fingers at Lily. His smile twisted into a grimace and he stood back to wink at her. Raising his hand into the air, he twisted it at an angle, appearing to be excited by this new ability.

Lily flung out her arms as her body rose from the ground, floating in mid-air. She cried out as Silas let her crash to the hard cobbles merely centimetres from the fire.

"Silas, stop." Mohana warned her son. Lightning lit up her corpse-like features.

"Stop? I've just discovered I have powers. So now I am teaching you a lesson. Magic is dangerous. It's witchcraft. I have just proved to you that your own magic can be used against you. It can cause mass destruction. It's evil. This is why I am about to destroy all of you." Silas's smirk dropped. A dark shadow cast over his warped features.

## NiNETEEN

# THE KEY TO FORGIVENESS

Eight fifty-seven. Three minutes. Harriet spun around when her muscles relaxed. Tyrone and Lily lay sprawled on the ground, barely moving. Lily's eyelids twitched. Tyrone's left shoe fidgeted. The fact they were moving was surely a good sign. At least they were alive. She turned three steps to face Silas. The possession happened when she got close to him.

All at once, she lost control of her muscles and her thoughts. Her black withered hair flapped wildly in the wind. She swept a strand of hair from her face and ran a finger across the deep wrinkles denting the right half of her skeletal face. She could still see through both her eyes, despite being able to poke a finger through the black holes where her eyes should've been.

Silas smirked. He glared at Mohana. "…What will you do now, *Mother*? You're all alone. You must regret sharing your powers with four others. Especially as one of them turned out to be me. Ha. You didn't see that coming, did you?"

"Oh, I don't regret sharing my powers at all. They will soon learn its true properties – to heal and produce charms," Mohana croaked. She paced closer to her son, despite the twisted grimace on his face. "I knew you would possess the jester. You had to pick on someone who was suffering just as you are. The boy needn't be burdened with your resentment as well as his own."

Silas tilted his head and stared into his mother's eyes. "You finished? What rubbish you speak. While your magic is still around, you and these youths are bringing evil into this village by working for the devil. As mayor, I had to have you executed; that is what the people wanted. It is what the King wanted. I had no choice but to listen. You made me do it."

Silas clenched his fist into a tight ball. All his pent-up fury gushed through his arms and he opened up his fists to expel a handful of rage at his mother.

An invisible force shoved Mohana backwards so fiercely that her legs flung above her chest. The end of the alleyway zoomed past her and she landed in a crumpled mess on the cobbles beside the fire. She should have flinched or screamed. Nothing. She couldn't react. She couldn't feel anything. It wasn't her body that was being wounded, but she couldn't let her host's body die. She needed it to finish this, to finally put this curse to rest.

Feet shifted behind her. She turned around. The other two friends staggered to their feet, gaping at her in a shocked silence.

"H… H… Harri?" The girl spoke faintly.

Mohana glared at them, her black hair beating in all directions as the storm grew violent. "Go to the graveyard and dig up his tomb. We will bring the bones. Hurry, we do not have long before our time is up. NOW."

The boy and girl didn't speak. They hesitated for a moment, not seeming sure whether to listen to her instruction. On checking her watch, the girl threw a frantic look at the boy and he shouted something. The two of them rushed through the Fair, in the direction of the graveyard.

Mohana rose to her feet and used her inner strength to pin Silas against the wall of the alleyway, imagining her fingers groping his throat so that he began to choke. "We all have choices."

Silas continued to fight for breath, grappling at his neck, his legs kicking out. An outburst of feral laughter twisted his mouth into something quite inhumane.

Mohana pressed harder and then released him. "Do you really want to carry on as you are? Full of all this anger, this hate? You are not a killer, Silas. You are a troubled man in need of love and approval. I hope you understand that I could not afford to keep you at home; I had to let you leave. All I could rely on was my magic to make me money. I failed you as a mother and I—"

"You killed me by infecting me with the Plague. I am sure that counts as failing me as a so-called mother. You chose your magic over me." Silas coughed; darkness hid his features. "As you have now witnessed, your magic is being used to hurt people. It is being used as a weapon."

Silas waited for Mohana to tread closer. Once she reached him, he slipped a hand into his waistcoat pocket and drew out a flaming ball of fire. He swung his arm around three times before lobbing it directly at Mohana's face.

She didn't flinch. The fireball shot straight into her open hand and she crushed it into a smattering of ashes, letting the remnants sprinkle to the floor. She took one step closer to her son. "As with any weapon, it is the responsibility of the user how they choose to control the weapon. Magic is strongly influenced by emotions, feelings; anger being the most dangerous – as it is with any form of *weapon*. You are currently controlling the villagers' thoughts and decisions with your curse, causing all this hatred and rage. You have brought back the Plague, which is now claiming the lives of those with poor health." Mohana reached out and held onto her son's shoulders. "This craving for revenge must stop now, son. Burning my bones will not end the curse. It is between you and me. There is no reason to involve these innocent people. What else is stopping you from moving on?"

"…I cannot forgive myself." Silas slackened at his mother's touch, at Harriet's touch, at his feelings, at Wayne's feelings. Was he beginning to weaken? His eyes switched from red to ice-blue, and he muttered under his breath in a husky East London accent. "I'm sorry, Mum."

Harriet's strength returned. Wayne was fighting to come back too. She wanted to ask if he was really there, when she quickly stopped herself, realising that now was the wrong moment. Was Silas about to forgive his mother now that Wayne had forgiven his? Harriet daren't move her eyes from Silas, not when they were so close to ending this. They needed to get a move on. One minute left.

Wayne's ice-blue eyes flicked from Harriet to the sack of bones in his hand. He swore at her through a pained expression. "Just take them. Quick. He's coming back."

Harriet chewed her lip. That was an order from Wayne, not Silas.

Something twitched in Wayne's face. His breathing deepened.

Harriet didn't bother wasting any more seconds. She grabbed the sack and raced back out of the alleyway.

Silas's eyes flashed red. He glared at Harriet. A demonic smile crept across his hard features.

*Come on, come on, you can do this*, Harriet swallowed hard. Without turning back, she sped along the slippery cobbles, through the derelict fair. Hailstones struck her face as she battled through the downpour of rain, splashing through the obstacle of puddles leading out of the Fair.

Heavy shoes raced across the cobbles a few metres behind her.

*He's catching up*, Harriet breathed. She forced her legs to move faster, even though it hurt to put her weight on them. She couldn't stop. The church had just come into view. The moon shone its blue rays onto the overgrown graveyard surrounding the church. The lit-up clock ticked eight fifty-nine. A stream of phlegm gurgled up her throat.

Just as she darted past the seesaw ride, her foot skidded on a cobble and she tumbled forwards onto her blistered hands, shrieking at the pain.

Silas drew closer, kicking a puddle in her face. His eyes switched between red and ice-blue. Wayne was battling to come back. His strengths were Silas's weakness: loyalty, protectiveness… heart. Perhaps he needed something to coax those feelings back out? Perhaps he'd already found something, otherwise he wouldn't be fighting so hard. Deep down, Harriet wanted to believe that she was the catalyst.

She crawled to her feet and limped closer to

the church. Tears pricked her eyes at the sight of Lily and Tyrone waiting there for her, frantically beckoning her towards them. They'd managed to grab a shovel from somewhere and in the time she'd been possessed by Mohana, they'd dug up the cracked grave with the carved man's hand that she'd seen on the first night. A huge heap of earth was piled up on one side. They stood beside the heap, staring down into the grave in question. She knew Lily wouldn't let her down.

The church clock struck its first peal, signifying the arrival of nine o'clock.

"Harri, come on!" Tyrone yelled, leaping on the spot.

One final stretch. Harriet squirmed at the pain in her hands and legs, driving her body forwards. Ahead, the trees began to spread out. A narrow slope of rocky slabs led Harriet down to the main graveyard. She clasped the sack tightly and dragged her feet the final few steps towards the grave at the back.

"Throw the bones in, Harri. Silas's bones already are in there. He is behind you!" Lily screeched.

Harriet leant over the grave and allowed Mohana's bones to roll from the sack and drop into the hollow ditch.

Silas stormed towards her but only reached as far as halfway when he couldn't walk any further due to the extremely slow rate his legs were moving. Something was happening to him.

Harriet peered over the ditch. The bottom looked miles away. Through the darkness, she could make out Silas's cracked bones lying flat in the open wooden coffin. Mohana's bones lay in a twisted heap squashed between the coffin and the earth where she had chucked them.

"They are not at peace yet. Wayne is still possessed by Silas. You are still having Mohana inside you too." Lily clutched her rosary beads.

Harriet paused. "We all need to forgive and be at peace with our pasts – not just Silas and Mohana. The four of us need to work together, to unite, as a team. We need Wayne back. And those bones down there, they need to be together," said Harriet. It was like she'd just slotted the last jigsaw piece into place.

Something heavy fell on top of her.

Before she had time to grab Lily for support, her foot skidded and she slipped over the edge of the ditch; the heavy thing flung an arm around her neck. Lily and Tyrone's shouts grew fainter as she fell feet-first down the black hole, her hands scraping against the mud and stones, struggling to cling on to something. The arm pressed tighter against her throat. She retched, trying to swallow. She could hear Silas rasping in her ear. The landing hit her hard. Her foot twisted in the wrong direction and she howled, tumbling into the coffin on top of Silas's bones. A patch of blood soaked through her jeans where she'd cut the skin on her leg on the way down. She tried to stand up. It hurt too much.

Harriet realised that both her and Wayne were down there together. They had to get out of here. Alive. She had to get Wayne back. Silas and Mohana had to forgive each other. She had to forgive Wayne.

"Wayne, come on, I know you're in there. You don't need Silas to get you through hard times. That's what friends are for," said Harriet, flinching when she moved her broken foot. She gazed into his eyes, blurting out what her heart was telling her, rather than her head. "That's… that's what I'm here for. I… I miss you."

Silas looked directly into her eyes. His breathing grew shallow. His face morphed into an oval shape. Eyes flicked between red and ice-blue. Water trickled from both eyes and his deep voice became husky. "I'm so sorry."

"Wayne?" Harriet became aware of tears rolling down her cheek.

His breaths were short, wheezy. Growling noises burbled in his chest, red eyes flickered. "I didn't want to hurt you, Mother. You gave me no choice. I was angry. I was angry that magic was more important to you than me."

"I forgive you." Harriet could hear her own voice blended in with Mohana's.

She raised her hand and let Silas rest his hand flat against hers, intertwining their fingers.

A gooey black liquid dribbled from Silas's mouth. His face crinkled, swelled and turned a dark shade of purple. Blood streamed from both nostrils. Red eyes faded to grey. Grey faded to white. White faded to ice-blue.

It's working! Harriet leant backwards and gently placed Mohana's bones beside Silas's bones in the coffin. She clasped their unbroken hands together and pulled the lid back over the top.

A grey haze drifted from Harriet and Wayne's bodies and headed upwards.

The clock struck its final ninth peal.

Harriet let out a breath and closed her eyes. She felt an arm wrap around her shoulders and another slide beneath her folded knees, lifting her up off the ground, taking the weight from her sore legs. She winced.

"You're gonna be alright. I've got you," said a voice that sounded like Wayne. She nodded, to which he whispered, "Make a wish to get us out."

Harriet did as he said.

The moment they returned to the top of the ditch beside Lily and Tyrone, they worked together to pile all the earth back into the ditch until it had been smoothed down at the top.

It looked like it'd never been touched.

The crack in the grave cemented together. A woman's carved hand emerged in the stone, her fingers cupped around the engraving of the man's hand.

"*We must all be at one for us to rest. Mine is his. His is mine. Our bones shall rest together. Kapayi,*

*Nihoyi. Vish hol luminar vos sorcerati.* Their spirits are at peace," Harriet said. A huge heaviness lifted from her. She felt lighter, positive, relieved.

A muffled cry resounded above the hilltops. The gallows dissolved into nothing. The muffled cries stopped. Then silence.

The first set of fireworks exploded across the skies beyond the village, announcing the beginning of November. Halloween was over at long last.

Harriet collapsed onto her knees. Was it really all over? Were they back in Bellsbury again? She cuddled her legs, burying her face in her knees. She could hear footsteps clip-clopping in her direction. A pair of slender arms cuddled her shoulders. Lips gently kissed her forehead.

"Hattie, what on earth?" Mum stroked the mud from Harriet's hair, kissing her head again. "I think we'd better get you to A&E, don't you?"

For once, the name Hattie didn't bother her anymore.

# TWENTY

# MOONSHINE WARD

Harriet rolled onto her back, staring up at the white tiled ceiling. It wasn't her bed. It didn't feel like her soft bed. The walls were the wrong colour too. Where was her silver clock and the purple lamp that usually sat on her desk? Even the bay window had disappeared and what was that weird smell? It was like a combination of bleach and antiseptic stuff. Those health magazines didn't belong to her either. Harriet tried to sit up when a tearing pain seared through her legs. A small cry left her lips. Everything hurt. She couldn't move. *Where am I?*

She could just about lift her head. Opposite her were three other beds occupied by children younger than her; one of them was a posh boy groaning that he'd been waiting for a nurse for half an hour. *A nurse?* She glanced beside her at the jug of water sitting on a bedside table to the sign above the doorway on the left reading 'Moonshine Ward'.

Last night's events suddenly came flooding back to her. Mum called an ambulance soon after everything went back to normal. Harriet had said goodbye to her friends as the paramedics carried her away on a stretcher, but they didn't go with her. Perhaps their injuries weren't as bad as hers. *Oh God, will I ever walk again?*

Her phone watch said nine-thirty in the morning. She rubbed the sleep from her eyes; not that she'd had much sleep these last few days. The screen lit up and a message popped up.

*Ping. Ping. Ping.*

She tapped open the app and smiled on seeing Lily's name. It looked like she'd created a group chat with two other people. Harriet peered closer. The two other people were Tyrone Stiles and Wayne Barry. Harriet's heart sped up to the point she thought it might explode. She gulped back her breaths, the mobile quivering in her sweaty hands.

**Lily**
Hey, just checking. Is everyone OK? Xx

**Wayne**
Dunno. You?

**Tyrone**

Didn't sleep. Feel well weird

**Lily**

Me too. I am so glad it's over. Yaya has just made me a nice breakfast xxxxxxxxx

**Wayne**

Sweet. What time shall I be there? ;-)

**Lily**

LOL. Maybe we all should meet up? Harri, are you still in hospital hun? Are you OK? Xx

*Harriet Price left the group.*

Harriet let her head sink back into her pillow, her muscles tense. She couldn't do it. Even just looking at Wayne's name, his profile picture, brought all the trauma back. Everything she'd felt the last few days was exactly how she was feeling right now. She knew it wasn't his fault. The others had forgiven him, so why couldn't she? Mohana had just taught her all about forgiveness. Had it all been for nothing? Perhaps she could write him a message, explaining how she was feeling. At least then he wouldn't think she was just being plain rude. Actually, she'd planned it all in her head, what she wanted to say. She'd been going over and over it in the ambulance, struggling to find the nerve to draft out the message and send it. She felt ready now.

Hastily, she tapped on Wayne's Facebook profile page and hit the message button, drawing in a long, shaky breath. *Here goes*, she whispered.

**Harriet**

Hi Wayne, hope you're OK. You know when you told me that every time you trust someone they mess with your head? Does the fact that I trusted you make me a twat? (Your words, not mine, right?) For once, I just want to be treated with respect instead of being used xxx

Harriet clicked 'send', squirming inside as she read it back to herself. It wasn't exactly what she'd planned to say. She shouldn't have put so many kisses. Was it too much? Wayne hadn't read the message yet. His online status read 'Active 20 minutes ago'. Guess she'd just have to wait. The longer she lay there, the twitchier every muscle in her body became. Her stomach rolled and flipped, flipped and rolled so much that she thought she might throw up. Never before had she checked Facebook Messenger so many times in the space of fifteen minutes.

Oh God. His status changed to 'Active now'. Minutes later, his profile photo appeared beneath her message. Oh heck, he was reading it. A bubble soon popped up below her message showing three bouncing dots. Her heart felt close to bursting. He was typing something.

*Ping.*

**Wayne**

I will reply mate. Don't want you to think I'm ignoring you. Hello by the way

**Wayne**

...

*He's actually going to reply*, Harriet breathed. Although if she lay here staring at this screen anymore, her head would explode. As if he could read her mind, he began typing. Another bubble with three dots popped up. It stopped for several moments and carried on. Wayne was writing something back. Harriet cleared the dryness in her throat. Across the aisle, a couple of nurses drew the curtains around the posh boy who'd been moaning about them. Now that he had their attention, he began moaning about the lack of computer magazines instead.

*Ping.*

**Wayne**

I get it and I'm sorry. Maybe my/Silas's behaviour made you think I weren't a true friend or I didn't care, but truth is, you're one of the nicest twats I've ever met ;-) Hate that you thought I was using you.

I wasn't. I'm not. I've got to live with what I've done, but hey, that's my life at the moment lol. Look after yourself, mate x

Before Harriet could reply, Wayne's status changed to offline. He probably had better things to do. Still, at least he replied to her. He'd even added a kiss! That warm flutter she'd felt when he first walked into their chamber came bounding back. She let her head relax back into the soft pillow, closing her eyes to the bustling footsteps, the noisy kids, the squeaking trolley wheels, the beeping monitors and the constant buzz of the nurse call buttons.

She let out a breath. She couldn't think about anything right now, not Wayne, not her friends, not even the magic. It hurt her head too much. She could only hope that things would get better.

# TWENTY-ONE

# BENEATH THE MASKS

Harriet turned left out of Borough Underground Station and headed towards the skate park hidden beneath the arches of the railway bridge. A sharp twinge fired up her leg and she groaned. The doctor said her ankle should heal within six to eight weeks. He said she'd twisted it pretty badly. More like dropped from a great height and hurled about. She just couldn't bear to spend another day sitting at home with her leg raised, watching rubbish TV.

A wintry breeze nipped at her face and she buried her chin into the woolly green scarf that Nan had knitted for her. Her hair flapped against her face as she paced through Borough Market, drinking in the explosion of fresh fruit, fish, sausages, curry and pastries. It took her straight back to Shire Square Market.

It'd been one month since what had happened at Bellsbury. She'd left hospital the next day looking like an Egyptian mummy. Mum was completely oblivious to what had happened after she'd turned evil. In fact, nobody at Bellsbury remembered a thing. Good thing was, all the staff and guests who'd died from the Plague had come back to life on that Halloween night. Lily believed that people who died by magic could be brought back by magic. They'd all agreed not to use their magic while they were apart. After what'd happened at Bellsbury, they realised that they needed each other. Only now it worried Harriet that she might've forgotten how to control it.

Apart from seeing Lily at school, Harriet hadn't seen the boys, or even spoken with them. Lily had kept her updated with the latest gossip. She spoke to the boys regularly via WhatsApp. Apparently, Tyrone spent a lot of his Saturdays helping his dad with roofing work. Wayne had moved back in with his mum and sister. The thought of seeing Wayne made Harriet nervous. They hadn't spoken to each other since their last exchange of messages at the hospital. She worried that seeing Wayne would bring the trauma back. Mum suggested she meet up with him. Speaking of Mum, she'd chosen not to see Ben again after the festival was over. The incidents surrounding

Harriet, and Dad's absence, seemed to have shaken her up a bit. Perhaps it made her reassess what was important. She never admitted whether anything had happened between her and Ben, but she'd changed. She'd become more present, more involved. She was really trying to make an effort with Dad.

Lily organised this catch-up only last week. She said it'd be something to look forward to before Christmas. The skate park was Tyrone's choice. It was only two minutes from his house and both he and Wayne were proficient skaters.

Harriet hobbled awkwardly beneath the archway that led her into the viaduct that'd been turned into a skate park. Graffiti covered the brickwork, the ramps and the staggered ledges that surrounded her. She paused to straighten her crutch, her bandaged leg beginning to ache. She could hear Lily's laughter from somewhere inside. She paused. Her heart rate soared to what felt like one million beats per second. Maybe she should turn around and go home.

"Harri!" Lily beamed, racing to fling her arms around Harriet and guiding her inside. It took some getting used to seeing her without her glasses. She'd started wearing contact lenses to stop the habit of tipping her glasses up her nose every few seconds. "Are you OK, chick? You are looking so beautiful."

"Mmm." Harriet couldn't even spit her words out properly. She took three deep breaths. "I'm OK, Lils. Have you been here long?"

"No, I came only ten minutes ago. The boys have been a while here," said Lily, resting her head on Harriet's shoulder and squeezing her arm.

Harriet turned at the sound of ripping, hollow scrapes and clickety-clack noises. She just about caught Wayne crouched on his board, skating down a big ramp. Just as he rolled upwards, he jumped in the air and somehow turned his board 360 degrees, landing back on it with both feet to the other side. Tyrone whooped at him from the opposite end, wriggling his own board from left to right. It was weird to think that only last month Wayne had been possessed by a spirit from the seventeenth century.

Lily's sudden yelp made Harriet flinch. "Tyrone, Wayne! Harri is here!"

Harriet was about to tell Lily she shouldn't have interrupted them until both boys paused to look down at her. *Oh God, he's seen me.* She swallowed hard. They waved and skated towards her. Wayne didn't look the same as he had when Harriet last saw him. Happier, a little fuller, untroubled. Tyrone seemed his usual laid-back self. She recalled finding him really annoying when he first stepped into their chamber. He was actually pretty cool.

"Hey, buddy, you alright?" Wayne greeted Harriet with a half-smile.

Tyrone clapped a hand on her shoulder. "What's up, dude?"

Wayne's eyes sidled down to Harriet's crutches

and bandaged leg. His smile disappeared and he looked up at her, mouthing, "I'm so sorry."

"It's OK." Harriet couldn't stop her voice from faltering. It was all coming back: the feelings, the pain, the hurt. Wayne must've sensed something because he used his foot to flip his skateboard into his arm and skulked off to sit on a step in the corner.

A rush of disappointment settled in the bottom of Harriet's stomach. That's not how she'd imagined her first conversation with Wayne would go. She hadn't known what to expect, but more than that at least. She'd barely said two words to him. She'd forgotten how to talk to him and had to get to know him all over again. *Be strong. Emotion is a power in itself. Magic, be it good or evil, can never influence one's true feelings. Trust and forgiveness is the key. Always follow your heart.* That wasn't a warning this time. It was an instruction. Even though Mohana had left Harriet's body, she still heard her words sometimes, like she had just now. Harriet found herself nodding, then grabbed her crutches and limped in the direction of Wayne. She had to tell him how she felt. She had to go after him.

"I'll be back in a second," Harriet called over her shoulder.

"If you're doing what I think you're doing, then you'll be longer than a second," said Tyrone, nudging Lily with a grin. "We'll just wait here."

"I'm going to check Wayne's OK, that's all," Harriet quickly cut in, hoping that Tyrone's comment hadn't triggered any resentment in Lily. To Harriet's surprise, Lily said nothing. She remained silent and pretended to wipe some dirt from Tyrone's skateboard.

Harriet paused. Wasn't it about time she stopped putting Lily's feelings before her own? She had nothing to feel guilty about. Other people's jealousy was not her problem – even her best friend's. Lily would just have to get over it. Harriet turned her attention to Wayne and hobbled towards him. He sat on a step, plucking the strings of an acoustic guitar resting against his leg. If she was being honest with herself, she had no idea what she was doing or what she was hoping to get out of it. It's like something had suddenly taken over. Except this time, it wasn't Mohana. It was confidence. It was feelings.

"You never told me you could play the guitar." She broke the silence.

Wayne looked up at her. "I can also snort milk up my nose and squirt it out my eye, but I never told you that either."

She'd actually missed that. She'd missed him. Had he missed her, she wondered? "That's gross! Can you play me something?"

"Sure, why not. If I'm playing, you're singing: them's the rules." Wayne tilted his head with a casual shrug. He lifted the guitar onto his lap, placed his fingers on the neck and began strumming. After the first few bars he glanced up at Harriet and hummed, waiting for her to recognise the tune. When he nodded for her to sing, she knew it straight away.

'Lavender's Blue'! She grinned to herself. This time, she didn't hesitate. Embarrassment wasn't even a thing right now. She opened her mouth and sang with the same gentle tone as before. It felt surprisingly natural. Wayne nodded reassuringly while he played along to her pace; she relaxed and held his gaze. Her cheeks heated up when his lips creased into a huge, dimpled smile. He finished the song by fingerpicking the last few strings and stopped to applaud Harriet, whistling with his fingers.

"Can't sing? Yeah, whatever." His eyes slanted down and crinkled at the edges as he watched her do a little curtsey, turning Harriet's insides into mush. He slid the guitar to the ground and budged up so that Harriet could sit on the step beside him.

Her stomach started performing star jumps. She'd never been this close to him – well, not since she drowned and he rescued her. That didn't count. He hadn't any choice. She stared into her lap, bouncing her knees up and down.

Wayne gave her a playful nudge. "You alright?"

Harriet smiled and nudged him back. "…Wayne? Do you mind, erm, can I ask you something?"

He leant back on his elbows and looked at her. "What's up?"

"I… did… you… erm… do you really think I look like that balloon witch you made?" Harriet blurted out. She kicked herself inside. That's not exactly what she'd planned to say.

Wayne restrained a bemused laugh.

This wasn't going well at all. She stared down at the floor. Wayne probably thought she was a joke, although he'd stopped teasing now.

He broke the silence. "No is the answer to your question. You're much taller."

Harriet giggled, lightly slapping his arm. She could see him more clearly now. It bothered her that his checked shirt collar poked up at different angles. She turned to face him and reached forwards, using both hands to fold his collar down, resting her hands on his shoulders when she'd finished. He didn't seem to mind that she was practically lying on him. She couldn't tear her eyes away from his lightly freckled face: those sparkling ice-blue eyes, his dimpled smile, that small stud in his ear.

Wayne whispered to her, "I've gotta say, you're insanely pretty for a witch."

Harriet bit her lip. "I bet you say that to all the girls."

"Actually, no. I've never been out with a witch." Wayne's expression was blank.

Harriet chuckled, then stopped herself; images from the banquet came flooding back. "But what about Jazz?"

"I've never said it to her either." Wayne regarded her closely.

"No, I mean do… do you think she's pretty?" Harriet regretted asking.

"She's overrated." His eyes were playful, and he waited for a moment. "You ask some weird questions. What else do you want to know? My shoe size?"

Harriet gazed at him and let her crutches clang to the floor. She didn't remember wrapping her arms around Wayne's waist or him stroking her hair from her bruised face. His Mohican hair felt so fluffy, his broad dimpled cheeks soft. But what happened next would stay in her mind forever. His lips pressed against hers. A million fireworks exploded inside her. When the kiss ended, she nestled her head beneath Wayne's chin and he gave her the longest, most comforting cuddle in the world, pressing his lips against her forehead. No stomach pains this time, but a wave of silent apologies passed between them. Her main wish had come true without having to use any magic.

"We good then, yeah?" Wayne curbed a broadening smile.

"Yeah." Harriet couldn't feel her legs anymore, and that wasn't down to the bandage.

A sudden cheer blasted from behind them. Tyrone pumped his fist in the air and made a noise that drunk men make when their favourite football team score a goal. "About time. You had the whole three days in Bellsbury to do this."

"Yeah. Problem was, I was possessed by Silas, and Harri was possessed by Mohana. In what kind of messed-up relationship does a son get off with his mother? There's a name for that," said Wayne to a chorus of laughter.

That was the first time they'd mentioned it and laughed about it. Wayne's joke had lifted a weight that'd burdened them for a whole month. They'd needed this. Togetherness. Trust. Forgiveness. That's the true magic, the true key that held a friendship together, a family together. That's what Mohana had been trying to drill into Harriet's head for three days. Had it not been for Mohana, perhaps she still wouldn't be speaking to Mum. Wayne might not have moved back to Stepney with his mum. Harriet might not have found the confidence to approach Wayne and sing to him!

"We were waiting to tell you that the pizza has arrived," Lily exclaimed, holding a foil tray loaded with hot, steaming pizza slices. She strolled over to the steps where Harriet was still laying on Wayne and stood directly in front of her.

Harriet swallowed; the anticipation of what was to come out of Lily's mouth made every muscle in her body tense up.

"Please. Have some pizza, both of you," Lily said finally, managing a grin.

Harriet let her muscles relax, a smile spreading across her face.

Her friends were on it like flies!

"Here's to Christmas! And to new friendship!"

Harriet raised her pizza slice in the air, tomato dripping onto her lap.

"To Christmas! And to new friendship!" Lily, Wayne and Tyrone lifted whatever was in their hands at the time; in Tyrone's case it was a half-eaten banana.

Harriet raised her hand and let her friends rest their hands flat against hers, intertwining their fingers. A blast of energy crossed between their hands. *The magic's only just begun. This is not the end*, the inner voice whispered.

# ACKNOWLEDGEMENTS

Twenty years ago, the spark of an idea that became *Hexed* was born. The story has been on an incredible journey through narrow alleyways, a maze of dark streets leading in every possible direction, until it was finally led to a place of magic. And now follows a huge witchy THANK YOU to all those who helped make it glisten and shine.

Chloe May, Fern Bushnell, Daniel Burchmore and the Editorial and Marketing team at The Book Guild for embracing Harriet and friends with open arms, engraving their words onto these pages and allowing them to finally share their story with you, their first audience. You've brought my dream to life!

Special thanks to my Golden Egg Academy family. My mentor, Tilda Johnson, nurtured Harriet's story for six years with her expert editorial guidance and passion. Without her, Harriet and friends may not have found their way out of that crumbling, dark dungeon!

Imogen Cooper and my lovely egg friends for their support and kindness these last few years. Also, to Vanessa Harbour for accepting me into The Golden Egg Academy in 2015 and seeing the potential in *Hexed*.

To Katherine, Sandra and Lorna at Cornerstones Literary Consultancy for looking through the earlier versions of *Hexed* and encouraging a lot of the ideas that have made it into the story today. Thank you for starting me off on this exciting adventure!

Before *Hexed* hatched out of its shell, thank you to some of its first readers, Louise Markham, Paul Macklin, Christopher Keddie, Jessica Nelson, Rus Madon and Kim Parker – thank you for your valuable feedback, encouragement and ongoing support and friendship through this exciting journey.

Stephen Clarke, thank you for the wonderful digital artwork you produced of Harriet and friends using descriptions from the story and random images I found on the internet! Your artwork is now printed nicely on my coffee mug.

To my crazy friend, Jorge Martínez, and my cousin-in-law, Raquel Zamora Martínez for checking Lily's Spanish dialogue was accurate. Thank you so much for always doing this without question, regardless of the bizarre dialogue I asked you to check! You are both superstars! Muchas gracias y todos los besos en el mundo!

To my fellow performer, Jack Charlesworth – now no longer a cheeky 16-year-old, but your teenage insights, support and valued time helped me step into the minds of my characters. Also, thanks to Xander Owers, Elena Constantinos and Charli-Ann Rogers for portraying my characters in a short film clip created for my ongoing research. You were perfect.

To my radio boss and fellow presenter, James Jones, for the promotion and support on my journey through publication. You'll never know how much I appreciate it!

I feel lucky to have worked at Madame Tussauds London. It gifted me with so many fresh ideas and knowledge about life in a working attraction. Those morning briefings in Premiere Nights were always an energetic start to the day!

I gathered inspiration from visiting The British Library, Roots and Grooves in Colchester, The Clink Prison Museum, St Dunstan in the East Church Garden, The London Dungeon, Colchester Castle Dungeons, Dorset, The Shambles in York and Hellfire Caves. These places helped me bring Bellsbury to life!

To all my wonderful friends and family – a huge thank you for all your ongoing support and patience while I've taken you on this crazy journey with me. Every one of you have inspired me in your own way. Making you proud and hearing that you've bought copies means the world!

To Luke, for believing in me and my writing. For putting up with my outbursts of laughter when reading sections of my own book. For always offering to read the many versions of *Hexed* since the dark ages – and for letting me have a dog.

And finally, the biggest THANK YOU goes to you, my reader. You have breathed life into these pages and made this journey worthwhile. It is now part of you as it is me. If you have found a part of yourself within these chapters, then that is the true magic key. I hope the story remains with you for some time to come. Perhaps not the curse!